Bayard Taylor

Home Pastorals, Ballads and Lyrics

Bayard Taylor

Home Pastorals, Ballads and Lyrics

ISBN/EAN: 9783744766081

Printed in Europe, USA, Canada, Australia, Japan

Cover: Foto ©Andreas Hilbeck / pixelio.de

More available books at **www.hansebooks.com**

HOME PASTORALS,

BALLADS AND LYRICS.

BY

BAYARD TAYLOR.

BOSTON:

JAMES R. OSGOOD AND COMPANY,

LATE TICKNOR & FIELDS, AND FIELDS, OSGOOD, & CO.

1875.

University Press: Welch, Bigelow, & Co.,
Cambridge.

AD AMICOS.

———◆———

SOMETIMES an hour of Fate's serenest weather
   Strikes through our changeful sky its coming beams;
Somewhere above us, in elusive ether,
   Waits the fulfilment of our dearest dreams.

So, when the wayward time and gift have blended,
   When hope beholds relinquished visions won,
The heavens are broken and a blue more splendid
   Holds in its bosom an enchanted sun.

Then words unguessed, in faith's own shyness guarded,
   To ears unused their welcome music bear:
Then hands help on that doubtingly retarded,
   And love is liberal as the Summer air.

The thorny chaplet of a slow probation
   Becomes the laurel Fate so long denied;
The form achieved smiles on the aspiration,
   And dream is deed and Art is justified!

Ah, nevermore the dull neglect, that smothers
  The bard's dependent being, shall return;
Forgotten lines are on the lips of others,
  Extinguished thoughts in other spirits burn!

Still hoarded lives what seemed so spent and wasted,
  And echoes come from dark or empty years;
Here brims the golden cup, no more untasted,
  But fame is dim through mists of grateful tears.

I sang but as the living spirit taught me,
  Beat towards the light, perchance with wayward wing;
And still must answer, for the cheer you 've brought me:
  I sang because I could not choose but sing.

From that wide air, whose greedy silence swallows
  So many voices, even as mine seemed lost,
I hear you speak, and sudden glory follows,
  As from a falling tongue of Pentecost.

So heard and hailed by you, that, standing nearest,
  Blend love with faith in one far-shining flame,
I hold anew the earliest gift and dearest, —
  The happy Song that cares not for its fame!

B T.

CONTENTS.

———•———

ODES.

HOME PASTORALS.

I

Λ

HOME PASTORALS.

———•———

PROËM.

Now, when the mocking-bird, returned from his
    Florida winter,
Sings where the sprays of the elm first touch the plumes
    of the cypress ;
When on the southern porch the stars of the jessamine
    sparkle
Faint in the dusk of leaves ; and the thirsty ear of the
    Poet
Calls for the cup of song himself must mix ere it
    gladden, —
Careful vintager first, though latest guest at the banquet, —
Where shall he turn ? What foreign Muse invites to her
    vineyard ?
Out of what bloom of the Past the wine of remoter roman-
    ces ?

Foxy our grapes, of earthy tang and a wildwood astrin-
gence
Unto fastidious tongues ; but later, it may be, their
juices,
Mellowed by time, shall grow to be sweet on the palates
of others.
So will I paint in my verse the forms of the life I am
born to,
Not mediæval, or ancient ! For whatso hath palpable
colors,
Drawn from being and blood, nor thrown by the spectrum
of Fancy,
Charms in the Future even as truth of the Past in the
Present.

.

II.

Not for this, nor for nearer voices of intimate counsel,—
When were ever they heeded? — but since I am sated
with visions,
Sated with all the siren Past and its rhythmical phantoms,
Here will I seek my songs in the quiet fields of my
boyhood,
Here, where the peaceful tent of home is pitched for a
season.

High is the house and sunny the lawn : the capes of the
   woodlands,
Bluff, and buttressed with many boughs, are gates to the
   distance
Blue with hill over hill, that sink as the pausing of music.
Here the hawthorn blossoms, the breeze is blithe in the
   orchards,
Winds from the Chesapeake dull the sharper edge of the
   winters,
Letting the cypress live, and the mounded box, and the
   holly ;
Here the chestnuts fall and the cheeks of peaches are
   crimson,
Ivy clings to the wall and sheltered fattens the fig-tree.
North and South are as one in the blended growth of the
   region,
One in the temper of man, and ancient, inherited habits.

III.

Yet, though fair as the loveliest landscapes of pastoral
   England,
Who hath touched them with song ? and whence my
   music, and whither ?

Life still bears the stamp of its early struggle and labor,
Still is shorn of its color by pious Quaker repression,
Still is turbid with calm, or only swift in the shallows.
Gone are the olden cheer, the tavern-dance and the fox-
　　hunt,
Muster at trainings, buxom lasses that rode upon pillions,
Husking-parties and jovial home-comings after the wed-
　　ding,
Gone, as they never had been!—and now, the serious
　　people
Solemnly gather to hear some wordy itinerant speaker
Talking of Temperance, Peace, or the Right of Suffrage
　　for Women.
Sport, that once like a boy was equally awkward and rest-
　　less,
Sits with thumb in his mouth, while a petulant ethical
　　bantling
Struts with his rod, and threatens our careless natural
　　joyance.
Weary am I with all this preaching the force of example,
Painful duty to self, and painfuller still to one's neighbor,
Moral shibboleths, dinned in one's ears with slavering
　　unction,
Till, for the sake of a change, profanity loses its terrors.

IV.

Clearly, if song is here to be found, I must seek it
 within me:
Song, the darling spirit that ever asserted her freedom,
Soaring on sunlit wing above the clash of opinions,
Poised at the height of Good with a sweeter and lovelier
 instinct!
Call thee I will not, my life's one dear and beautiful
 Angel,
Wayward, faithful and fond; but, like the Friends in the
 Meeting,
Waiting, will so dispose my soul in the pastoral stillness,
That, denied to Desire, Obedience yet may invite thee!

MAY-TIME.

I.

YES, it is May! though not that the young leaf pushes
    its velvet
Out of the sheath, that the stubbornest sprays are
    beginning to bourgeon,
Larks responding aloft to the mellow flute of the bluebird,
Nor that song and sunshine and odors of life are im-
    mingled
Even as wines in a cup; but that May, with her delicate
    philtres
Drenches the veins and the valves of the heart, — a
    double possession,
Touching the sleepy sense with sweet, irresistible languor,
Piercing, in turn, the languor with flame: as the spirit,
    requickened,
Stirred in the womb of the world, foreboding a birth and
    a being!

1 *

II.

Who can hide from her magic, break her insensible
  thraldom,
Clothing the wings of eager delight as with plumage of
  trouble?
Sweeter, perchance, the embryo Spring, forerunner of
  April,
When on banks that slope to the south the saxifrage
  wakens,
When, beside the dentils of frost that cornice the road-
  side,
Weeds are a promise, and woods betray the trailing
  arbutus.
Once is the sudden miracle seen, the truth and its rapture
Felt, and the pulse of the possible May is throbbing
  already.
Thus unto me, a boy, the clod that was warm in the
  sunshine,
Murmurs of thaw, and imagined hurry of growth in the
  herbage,
Airs from over the southern hills, -- and something
  within me
Catching a deeper sign from these than ever the senses,—

Came as a call: I awoke, and heard, and endeavored to
answer.

Whence should fall in my lap the sweet, impossible marvel?

When would the silver fay appear from the willowy thicket?

When from the yielding rock the gnome with his basket of
jewels?

"When, ah when?" I cried, on the steepest perch of the
hillside

Standing with arms outspread, and waiting a wind that
should bear me

Over the apple-tree tops and over the farms of the valley.

III.

He, that will, let him backward set the stream of his fancy,

So to evoke a dream from the ruined world of his
boyhood!

Lo, it is easy! Yonder, lapped in the folds of the
uplands,

Bickers the brook, to warmer hollows southerly creeping,

Where the veronica's eyes are blue, the buttercup brightens,

Where the anemones blush, the coils of fern are unrolling

Hour by hour, and over them flutter the sprinkles of
shadow.

There shall I lie and dangle my naked feet in the water,

Watching the sleepy buds as one after one they awaken,

Seeking a lesson in each, a brookside primrose of Wordsworth ? —

Lie in the lap of May, as a babe that loveth the cradle,

I, whom her eye inspires, whom the breath of her passion
arouses ?

Say, shall I stray with bended head to look for her posies,

When with other wings than the coveted lift of the breezes

Far I am borne, at her call : and the pearly abysses are
parted   .

Under my flight : the glimmering edge of the planet,
receding,

Rounds to the splendider sun and ripens to glory of color.

Veering at will, I view from a crest of the jungled Antilles

Sparkling, limitless billows of greenness, falling and
flowing

Into fringes of palm and the foam of the blossoming
coffee, —

Cratered isles in the offing, milky blurs of the coral

Keys, and vast, beyond, the purple arc of the ocean :

Or, in the fanning furnace-winds of the tenantless Pampas,

Hear the great leaves clash, the shiver and hiss of the
reed-beds.

Thus for the crowded fulness of life I leave its begin-
    nings,
Not content to feel the sting of an exquisite promise
Ever renewed and accepted, and ever freshly forgotten.

IV.

Wherefore, now, recall the pictures of memory? Where-
    fore
Yearn for a fairer seat of life than this I have chosen?
Ah, while my quiver of wandering years was yet unex-
    hausted,
Treading the lands, a truant that wasted the gifts of his
    freedom,
Sweet was the sight of a home — or tent, or cottage, or
    castle, —
Sweet unto pain; and never beheld I a Highlander's
    shieling,
Never a Flemish hut by a lazy canal and its pollards,
Never the snowy gleam of a porch through Apennine
    orchards,
Never a nest of life on the hoary hills of Judæa,
Dropped on the steppes of the Don, or hidden in valleys
    of Norway,

But, with the fond and foolish trick of a heart that was
  homeless,
Each was mine, as I passed: I entered in and pos-
  sessed it,
Looked, in fancy, forth, and adjusted my life to the
  landscape.
Easy it seemed, to shift the habit of blood as a mantle,
Fable a Past, and lightly take the form of the Future,
So that a rest were won, a hold for the filaments,
  floating
Loose in the winds of Life.   Here, now, behold it accom-
  plished !
Nay, but the restless Fate, the certain Nemesis follows,
As to the bird the voice that bids him prepare for his
  passage,
Saying: " Not this is the whole, not these, nor any, the
  borders
Set for thy being ; this measured, slow repetition of
  Nature,
Painting, effacing, in turn, with hardly a variant outline,
Cannot replace for thee the Earth's magnificent frescos !
Art thou content to inhabit a simple pastoral chamber,
Leaving the endless halls of her grandeur and glory
  untrodden ? "

V.

Man, I answer, is more: I am glutted with physical
    beauty

Born of the suns and rains and the plastic throes of the
    ages.

Man is more; but neither dwarfed like a tree of the
    Arctic

Vales, nor clipped into shape as a yew in the gardens
    of princes.

Give me to know him, here, where inherited laws and
    disguises

Hide him at times from himself, — where his thought is
    chiefly collective,

Where, with numberless others fettered like slaves in a
    cofile,

Each insists he is free, inasmuch as his bondage is willing.

Who hath rent from the babe the primitive rights of his
    nature?

Who hath fashioned his yoke? who patterned beforehand
    his manhood?

Say, shall never a soul be moved to challenge its portion,

Seek for a wider heritage lost, a new disenthralment,

Sending a root to be fed from the deep original sources,

So that the fibres wax till they split the centuried granite?

Surely, starting alike at birth from the ignorant Adam,

Every type of the race were here indistinctly repeated,

Hinted in hopes and desires, and harmless divergence
    of habit,

Save that the law of the common mind is invisibly
    written

Even on our germs, and Life but warms into color the
    letters.

VI.

Thence, it may be, accustomed to dwen in a moving
    horizon,

Here, alas! the steadfast circle of things is a weary

Round of monotonous forms: I am haunted by livelier
    visions.

Linking men and their homes, endowing both with the
    language,

Sweeter than speech, the soul detects in a natural picture,

I to my varying moods the fair remembrances summon,

Glad that once and somewhere each was a perfect pos-
    session.

Two will I paint, the forms of the double passion of May-
    time, —

Rest and activity, indolent calm and the sweep of the
    senses.

One, the soft green lap of a deep Dalecarlian valley,

Sheltered by piny hills and the distant porphyry moun-
    tains ;

Low and red the house, and the meadow spotted with
    cattle ;

All things fair and clear in the light of the midsummer
    Sabbath,

Touching, beyond the steel-blue lake and the twinkle of
    birch-trees,

Houses that nestle like chicks around the motherly
    church-roof.

There, I know, there is innocence, ancient duty and
    honor,

Love that looks from the eye and truth that sits on the
    forehead,

Pure, sweet blood of health, and the harmless freedom
    of nature,

Witless of blame; for the heart is safe in inviolate child-
    hood.

Dear is the scene, but it fades : I see, with a leap of the
    pulses,

Tawny under the lidless sun the sand of the Desert,

Fiery solemn hills, and the burning green of the date-trees

Belting the Nile: the tramp of the curvetting stallions is
     muffled ;

Brilliantly stamped on the blue are the white and scarlet
     of turbans ;

Lances prick the sky with a starry glitter ; the fulness,

Joy, and delight of life are sure of the day and the
     morrow,

Certain the gifts of sense, and the simplest order suffices.

Breathing again, as once, the perfect air of the Desert,

Good it seems to escape from the endless menace of duty,

There, where the will is free, and wilfully plays with its
     freedom,

And the lack of will for the evil thing is a virtue.

VII.

Man is more, I have said: but the subject mood is a
     fashion

Wrought of his lighter mind and dyed with the hues of
     his senses.

Then to be truly more, to be verily free, to be master

As beseems to the haughty soul that is lifted by knowl-
     edge

Over the multitude's law, enforcing their own acquiescence, —

Lifted to longing and will, in its satisfied loneliness cen-
  tred, —

This prohibits the cry of the nerves, the weak lamentation

Shaming my song: for I know whence cometh its lan-
  guishing burden.

Impotent all I have dreamed, — and the calmer vision
  assures me

Such were barren, and vapid the taste of joy that is skin-
  deep.

Better the nest than the wandering wing, the loving
  possession,

Intimate, ever-renewed, than the circle of shallower
  changes.

AUGUST.

I.

DEAD is the air, and still! the leaves of the locust and walnut

Lazily hang from the boughs, inlaying their intricate outlines

Rather on space than the sky, — on a tideless expansion of slumber.

Faintly afar in the depths of the duskily withering grasses

Katydids chirp, and I hear the monotonous rattle of crickets.

Dead is the air, and ah! the breath that was wont to refresh me

Out of the volumes I love, the heartful, whispering pages,

Dies on the type, and I see but wearisome characters only.

Therefore be still, thou yearning voice from the garden in Jena, —

Still, thou answering voice from the park-side cottage in
  Weimar, —

Still, sentimental echo from chambers of office in Dres-
  den, —

Ye, and the feebler and farther voices that sound in the
  pauses !

Each and all to the shelves I return ; for vain is your
  commerce

Now, when the world and the brain are numb in the torpor
  of August.

II.

Over the tasselled corn, and fields of the twice-blossomed
  clover,

Dimly the hills recede in the reek of the colorless
  hazes :

Dull and lustreless, now, the burnished green of the
  woodlands ;

Leaves of blackberry briers are bronzed and besprinkled
  with copper ;

Weeds in the unmown meadows are blossoming purple
  and yellow,

Roughly entwined, a wreath for the tan and wrinkles of
  Summer.

Where shall I turn? What path attracts the indifferent
    footstep,
Eager no more as in June, nor lifted with wings as in
    May-time?
Whitherward look for a goal, when buds have exhausted
    their promise,
Harvests are reaped, and grapes and berries are waiting
    for Autumn?
Wander, my feet, as ye list! I am careless, to-day, to
    direct you.
Take, here, the path by the pines, the russet carpet of
    needles
Stretching from wood to wood, and hidden from sight by
    the orchard!
Here, in the sedge of the slope, the centuary, pink as a
    sea-shell,
Opens her stars all at once, and with finer than tropical
    spices
Sweetens the season's drouth, the censer of fields that are
    sterile.
Now, from the height of the grove, between the irregular
    tree-trunks,
Over the falling fields and the meadowy curves of the
    valley,

Glimmer the peaceful farms, the mossy roofs of the houses,
Gables gray of the neighboring barns, and gleams of the
  highway
Climbing the ridges beyond to dip in the dream of a forest.

III.

Ah, forsaking the shade, and slowly crushing the stubble,
Parting the viscous roseate stems and the keen penny-
  royal,
Rises a different scene, suggestion of heat and of still-
  ness, —
Heat as intense and stillness as dumb, the immaculate
  ether's
Hush when it vaults the waveless Mediterranean sea-floor;
Golden the hills of Cos, with pencilled cerulean shadows;
Phantoms of Carian shores that are painted and fade in
  the distance ;
Patmos behind, and westward the flushed Ariadnean
  Naxos, —
Once as I saw them sleeping, drugged by the poppy of
  Summer.
There, indeed, was the air, as with floating stars of the
  thistle

Filled with impalpable forms, regrets, possibilities, long-
       ings,
Beauty that was and was not, and Life that was rhythmic
       and joyous,
So that the sun-baked clay the peasant took for his wine-
       jars
Brighter than gold I thought, and the red acidity nectar.
Here, at my feet, the clay is clay and a nuisance the
       stubble,
Flaring St.-John's-wort, milk-weed, and coarse, unpoetical
       mullein ; —
Yet, were it not for the poets, say, is the asphodel
       fairer?
Were not the mullein as dear, had Theocritus sung it, or
       Bion?
Yea, but they did not ; and we, whose fancy's tenderest
       tendrils
Shoot unsupported, and wither, for want of a Past we can
       cling to,
We, so starved in the Present, so weary of singing the
       Future, —
What is 't to us, if, haply, a score of centuries later,
Milk-weed inspires Patagonian tourists, and mulleins are
       classic?

IV.

Idly balancing fortunes, feeling the spite of them,
　　maybe, —
For the little withheld outweighs the much that is given, —
Feeling the pang of the brain, the endless, unquenchable
　　yearning
Born of the knowledge of Beauty, not to be shared or
　　imparted,
Slowly I stray, and drop by degrees to the thickets of
　　alder
Fringing a couch of the stream, a basin of watery slumber.
Broken, it seems ; for the splash and the drip and the
　　bubbles betoken
What ? — the bath of a nymph, the bashful strife of a
　　Hylas ?
Broad is the back, and bent from an un-Olympian stoop-
　　ing,
Narrow the loins and firm, the white of the thighs and
　　the shoulders
Changing to reddest and toughest of tan at the knees and
　　the elbows.
Is it a faun? He sees me, nor cares to hide in the thickets.
Faun of the bog is he, a sylvan creature of Galway

2

Come from the ditch below, to cleanse him of sweat and
    of muck-stain ;
Willing to give me speech, as, naked, he stands in the
    shallows.
Something of coarse, uncouth, barbaric, he leaves on the
    bank there ;
Something of primitive human fairness cometh to clothe
    him.
Were he not bent with the pick, but straightened from
    reaching the bunches
Hung from the mulberry branches, — heard he the bac-
    chanal cymbals,
Took from the sun an even gold on the web of his muscles,
Knew the bloom of his stunted bud of delight of the
    senses, —
Then as faun or shepherd he might have been welcome in
    marble.
Yea, but he is not ; and I, requiring the beautiful balance,
Music of life in the body, and limbs too fair to be hidden,
Find, indeed, some delicate colors and possible graces, —
Moral hints of the man beneath the unsavory garments, —
Find them, and sigh, lamenting the law reversed of the
    races
Starting the world afresh on the basis unlovely of Labor.

V.

Was it a spite of fate that blew me hither, an exile,
Still unweaned, and not to be weaned, from the milk I was
  born to?
Bitter the stranger's bread to the homesick, hungering
  palate ;
Bitterer still to the soul the taste of the food that is foreign!
Yet must I take it, yet live, and somehow seem to be
  healthy,
Lest my neighbors, perchance, be shocked by an
  uncomprehended
Violent clamor for that which I crave and they cannot
  supply me, —
Hunger unmeet for the times, anachronistical passions, —
Beauty seeming distorted because the rule is distortion.
Here is a tangle which, now, too idle am I to unravel,
Snared, moreover, by bitter-sweet, moon-seed, and riotous
  fox-grape,
Meshing the thickets : *procul, O procul,* unpractical fancies!
Verily, thus bewildering myself in the maze of æsthetic,
Solveless problems, the feet were wellnigh heedlessly
  fettered.
Thoughtless, 't is true, I relinquished my books ; but

Wisely was said, — for desperate vacancy prompted the
　　ramble,
Memories prolonged, and a phantom of logic urges it
　　onward.

VI.

Here are the fields again !　The soldierly maize in tassel
Stands on review, and carries the scabbarded ears in its
　　arm-pits.
Rustling I part the ranks, — the close, engulfing battalions
Shaking their plumes overhead, — and, wholly bewildered
　　and heated,
Gain the top of the ridge, where stands, colossal, the
　　pin-oak.
Yonder, a mile away, I see the roofs of the village, —
See the crouching front of the meeting-house of the
　　Quakers,
Oddly conjoined with the whittled Presbyterian steeple.
Right and left are the homes of the slow, conservative
　　farmers,
Loyal people and true, but, now that the battles are
　　over,
Zealous for Temperance, Peace, and the Right of Suffrage
　　for Women.

Orderly, moral, are they, — at least, in the sense of
suppression ;

Given to preaching of rules, inflexible outlines of duty ;

Seeing the sternness of life, but, alas ! overlooking its
graces.

Let me be juster: the scattered seeds of the graces are
planted

Widely apart ; but the trumpet-vine on the porch is a
token ;

Yea, and awake and alive are the forces of love and
affection,

Plastic forces that work from the tenderer models of
beauty.

Who shall dare to speak of the possible ? Who shall
encounter

Pity and wrath and reproach, recalling the record
immortal

Left by the races when Beauty was law and Joy was
religion ?

Who to the Duty in drab shall bring the garlanded
Pleasure ? —

Break with the chant of the gods, the gladsome timbrels
of morning,

Nasal, monotonous chorals, sung by the sad congregation?

Better it were to sleep with the owl, to house with the
    hornet,
Than to conflict with the satisfied moral sense of the
    people.

VII.

Nay, but let me be just; nor speak with the alien language
Born of my blood ; for, cradled among them, I know them
    and love them.
Was it my fault, if a strain of the distant and dead
    generations
Rose in my being, renewed, and made me other than
    these are ?
Purer, perhaps, their habit of law than the freedom they
    shrink from ;
So, restricted by will, a little indulgence is riot.
They, content with the glow of a carefully tempered
    twilight,
Measured pulses of joy, and colorless growth of the
    senses,
Stand aghast at my dream of the sun, and the sound, and
    the splendor !
Mine it is, and remains, resenting the threat of suppres-
    sion,

Stubbornly shaping my life, and feeding with fragments its
     hunger.
Drifted from Attican hills to stray on a Scythian level,
So unto me it appears, — unto them a perversion and
     scandal.

VIII.

Lo! in the vapors, the sun, colossal and crimson and
     beamless,
Touches the woodland; fingers of air prepare for the
     dew-fall.
Life is fresher and sweeter, insensibly toning to softness
Needs and desires that are but the broidered hem of its
     mantle,
Not the texture of daily use ; and the soul of the land-
     scape,
Breathing of justified rest, of peace developed by
     patience,
Lures me to feel the exquisite senses that come from
     denial,
Sharper passion of Beauty never fulfilled in external
Forms or conditions, but always a fugitive has-been or
     may-be.
Bright and alive as a want, incarnate it dozes and fattens.

Thus, in aspiring, I reach what were lost in the idle
    possession ;

Helped by the laws I resist, the forces that daily depress
    me ;

Bearing in secreter joy a luminous life in my bosom,

Fair as the stars on Cos, the moon on the boscage of
    Naxos !

Thus the skeleton Hours are clothed with rosier bodies :

Thus the buried Bacchanals rise unto lustier dances :

Thus the neglected god returns to his desolate temple :

Beauty, thus rethroned, accepts and blesses her children !

NOVEMBER.

I.

WRAPPED in his sad-colored cloak, the Day, like a
Puritan, standeth

Stern in the joyless fields, rebuking the lingering
color, —

Dying hectic of leaves and the chilly blue of the
asters, —

Hearing, perchance, the croak of a crow on the desolate
tree-top,

Breathing the reek of withered weeds, or the drifted and
sodden

Splendors of woodland, as whoso piously groaneth in
spirit:

"Vanity, verily; yea, it is vanity, let me forsake it!

Yea, let it fade, for Life is the empty clash of a cymbal,

Joy a torch in the hands of a fool, and Beauty a
pitfall!"

2*   c

II.

Once, I remember, when years had the long duration of
  ages,
Came, with November, despair; for summer had vanished
  forever.
Lover of light, my boyish heart as a lover's was jealous,
Followed forsaking suns and felt its passion rejected,
Saw but Age and Death, in the whole wide circle of
  Nature
Throned forever; and hardly yet have I steadied by
  knowledge
Faith that faltered and patience that was but a weary
  submission.
Though to the right and left I hear the call of the huskers
Scattered among the rustling shocks, and the cheerily
  whistled
Lilt of an old plantation tune from an ebony teamster,
These behold no more than the regular jog of a mill-
  wheel
Where, unto me, there is possible end and diviner
  beginning.
Silent are now the flute of Spring and the clarion of
  Summer   .

As they had never been blown: the wail of a dull
Miserere

Heavily sweeps the woods, and, stifled, dies in the
valleys.

III.

Who are they that prate of the sweet consolation of
Nature?

They who fly from the city's heat for a month to the
sea-shore,

Drink of unsavory springs, or camp in the green Adiron-
dacks?

They, long since, have left with their samples of ferns and
of algæ,

Memories carefully dried and somewhat lacking in color,

Gossip of tree and cliff and wave and modest adventure,

Such as a graceful sentiment — not too earnest — admits
of,

Heard in the pause of a dance or bridging the gaps of a
dinner.

Nay, but I, who know her, exult in her profligate seasons,

Turn from the silence of men to her fancied, fond
recognition,

I am repelled at last by her sad and cynical humor.

Kinder, cheerier now, were the pavements crowded with
    people,
Walls that hide the sky, and the endless racket of busi-
    ness.
There a hope in something lifts and enlivens the current,
Face seeth face, and the hearts of a million, beating
    together,
Hidden though each from other, at least are outwardly
    nearer,
Lending the life of all to the one,—bestowing and taking,
Weaving a common web of strength in the meshes of
    contact,
Close, yet never impeded, restrained, yet delighting in
    freedom.
There the soul, secluded in self, or touching its fellow
Only with horny palms that hide the approach of the
    pulses,
Driven abroad, discovers the secret signs of its kindred,
Kisses on lips unknown, and words on the tongue of the
    stranger.
Life is set to a statelier march, a grander accordance
Follows its multitudinous steps of dance and of battle :
Part hath each in the music ; even the sacredest whisper
Findeth a soul unafraid and an ear that is ready to listen.

IV.

Nature? 'T is well to sing of the glassy Bandusian
    fountain,   •

Shining Ortygian beaches, or flocks on the meadows of
    Enna,

Linking the careless life with the careless mood of the
    Mother.

We, afar and alone, confronted with heavier questions,

Robbed of the oaten pipe before it is warm in our fingers,

Why should we feign a faith?—why crown an indifferent
    goddess?

Under the gray, monotonous vault what carolling song-
    bird

Hopes for an echo? Closer and lower the vapors are
    folded;

Sighing shiver the woods, though drifted leaves are
    unrustled;

Ghosts of the grasses that fled with a breath and floated
    in sunshine

Hang unstirred on brier and fence; for a new desolation

Comes with the rain, that, chilly and quietly creeping at
    nightfall,

Thence for many a day shall dismally drizzle and darken.

V.

" See ! " (methinks I hear the mechanical routine repeated,)
" Emblems of faith in the folded bud and the seed that is
     sleeping ! "
Knowledge, not Faith, deduced the similitude ; how shall
     an emblem
Give to the soul the steadfast truth that alone satisfies it ?
Joy of the Spring I can feel, but not the preaching of
     Autumn.
Earth, if a lesson is wrought upon each of thy radiant
     pages,
Give us the words that sustain us, and not the words that
     discourage !
Sceptic art thou become, the breeder of doubt and
     confusion,
Powerless vassal of Fate, assuming a meek resignation.   '
Yielding the forces that moved in thy life and made it
     triumphant !

VI.

Now, as my circle of home is slowly swallowed in
     darkness,
As with the moan of winds the rain is drearily falling, —

Hopes that drew as the sun and aims that stood as the
pole-star

Fading aloof from my life as though it never had known
them, —

Where, when the wont is deranged, shall I find a
permanent foothold?

Stripped of the rags of Time I see the form of my
being,

Born of all that ever has been, and haughtily reaching

Forward to all that comes, — yet certain, this moment, of
nothing.

Chide or condemn as ye may, the truant and mutinous
spirit

Turns on itself, and forces release from its holiest
habit;

Soars where the suns are sprinkled in cold, illimited
darkness,

Peoples the spheres with far diviner forms of existence,

Questions, conjectures at will; for Earth and its creeds
are forgotten.

Thousands of æons it gathers, yet scarce its feet are
supported;

Dumb is the universe unto the secrets of Whence? and of
Whither?

So, as a dove through the summits of ether falling
   exhausted,
Under it yawns the blank of an infinite Something — or
   Nothing!

VII.

Let me indulge in the doubt, for this is the token of
   freedom,
This is all that is safe from hands that would fain
   intermeddle,
Thrusting their worn phylacteries over the eyes that are
   seeking
Truth as it shines in the sky, not truth as it smokes in
   their lantern.
Ah, shall I venture alone beyond the limits they set us,
Bearing the spark within till a breath of the Deity fan it
Into an upward-pointing flame? — and, forever unquiet,
Nearer through error advance, and nearer through igno-
   rant yearning?
Yes, it must be: the soul from the soul cannot hide or
   diminish
Aught of its essence: here the duplicate nature is ended:
Here the illusions recede, at man's unassailable centre,
And the nearness and farness of God are all that is left
   him.

VIII.

Lo! as I muse, there come on the lonely darkness and
silence

Gleams like those of the sun that reach his uttermost
planet,

Inwardly dawning ; and faint and sweet as the voices of
waters

Borne from a sleeping mountain-vale on a breeze of the
midnight,

Falls a message of cheer : " Be calm, for to doubt is to
seek whom

None can escape, and the soul is dulled with an idle
acceptance.

Crying, questioning, stumbling in gloom, thy pathway
ascendeth ;

They with the folded hands at the last relapse into
strangers.

Over thy head, behold! the wing with its measureless
shadow

Spread against the light, is the wing of the Angel of
Unfaith,

Chosen of God to shield the eyes of men from His
glory.

Thus through mellower twilights of doubt thou climbest
     undazzled,
Mornward ever directed, and even in wandering guided.
God is patient of souls that reach through an endless
     creation,
So but His shadow be seen, but heard the trail of His
     mantle !"

IX.

Who is alone in this?   The elder brothers, immortal,
Leaned o'er the selfsame void and rose to the same
     consolation,
Human therein as we, however diviner their message.
Even as the liquid soul of summer, pent in the flagon,
Waits in the darksome vault till we crave its odor and
     sunshine,
So in the Past the words of life, the voices eternal.
Freedom like theirs we claim, yet lovingly guard in the
     freedom
Sympathies due to the time and help to the limited
     effort ;
Thus with double arms embracing our duplicate being,
Setting a foot in either world, we stand as the Masters.
Ah, but who can arise so far, except in his longing?

Give me thy hand! — the soft and quickening life of thy
    pulses
Spans the slackened spirit and lifts the eyelids of Fancy:
Doubt is of loneliness born, belief companions the lover.
Ever from thee, as once from youth's superfluous forces,
Courage and hope are renewed, the endless future created.
Out of the season's hollow the sunken sun shall be lifted,
Bringing faith in his beams, the green resurrection of
    Easter,
After the robes of death by the angels of air have been
    scattered,
Climbing the heights of heaven, to stand supreme at his
    solstice!

L'ENVOI.

I.

MAY-TIME and August, November, and over the
   winter to May-time,
Year after year, or shaken by nearness of imminent battle,
Or as remote from the stir as an isle of the sleepy Pacific,
Here, at least, I have tasted peace in the pauses of labor,
Rest as of sleep, the gradual growth of deliberate Nature.
Here, escaped from the conflict of taste, the confusion of
   voices
Heard in a land where the form of Art abides as a
   stranger,
Come to me definite hopes and clearer possible duties,
Faith in the steadfast service, content with tardy achieve-
   ment.
Here, in men, I have found the elements working as
   elsewhere,
Ever betraying the surge and swell of invisible currents,

Which, from beneath, from the deepest bases of thought
in the people,
Press, and heavy with change, and filled with visions
unspoken,
Bear us onward to shape the formless face of the Future.

II.

Now, if the tree I planted for mine must shadow another's,
If the uncounted tender memories, sown with the seasons,
Filling the webs of ivy, the grove, the terrace of roses,
Clothing the lawn with unwithering green, the orchard
with blossoms,
Singing a finer song to the exquisite motion of waters,
Breathing profounder calm from the dark Dodonian oak-
trees,
Now must be lost, till, haply, the hearts of others renew
them, —
Yet we have had and enjoyed, we have and enjoy them
forever.
Drops from the bough the fruit that here was sunnily
ripened:
Other will grow as well on the westward slope of the
garden.

Sorrowing not, nor driven forth by the sword of an angel,
Nay, but borne by a fuller tide as a ship from the harbor,
Slowly out of our eyes the pastoral bliss of the landscape
Fades, and is dim, and sinks below the rim of the ocean.

III.

Sorrowing not, I have said : with thee was the ceasing of
    sorrow.
Hope from thy lips I have drawn, and subtler strength
    from thy spirit,
Sharer of dream and of deed, inflexible conscience of
    Beauty!
Though as a Grace thou art dear, as a guardian Muse
    thou art earnest,
Walking with purer feet the paths of song that I venture,
Side by side, unwearied, in cheerful, encouraging silence.
Not thy constant woman's heart alone I have wedded ;
One are we made in patience and faith and high aspi-
    ration.
Thus, at last, the light of the fortunate age is recovered :
Thus, wherever we wander, the shrine and the oracle
    follow !

BALLADS.

BALLADS.

———•———

THE HOLLY-TREE.

I.

THE corn was warm in the ground, the fences were
    mended and made,
And the garden-beds, as smooth as a counterpane is laid,
Were dotted and striped with green where the peas and
    radishes grew,
With elecampane at the foot, and comfrey, and sage, and
    rue.

II.

The work was done on the farm, 't was orderly every-
    where,
And comfort smiled from the earth, and rest was felt in
    the air.
When a Saturday afternoon at such a time comes round,
The farmer's fancies grow, as grows the grain in his
    · ground.

III.

'T was so with Gabriel Parke : he stood by the holly-tree

That came, in the time of Penn, with his fathers over the
sea :

A hundred and eighty years it had grown where it first
was set,

And the thorny leaves were thick and the trunk was
sturdy yet.

IV.

From the knoll where stood the house the fair fields
pleasantly rolled

To dells where the laurels hung, and meadows of butter-
cup-gold :

He looked on them all by turns, with joy in his acres
free,

But ever his thoughts came back to the tale of the holly-
tree.

V.

In beautiful Warwickshire, beside the Avon stream,

John Parke, in his English home, had dreamed a singular
dream.

He went with a sorrowful heart, for love of a bashful
maid,

And a vision came as he slept one day in a holly's
shade.

VI.

An angel sat in the boughs, and showed him a goodly
land,

With hills that fell to a brook, and forests on either
hand,

And said: "Thou shalt wed thy love, and this shall
belong to you ;

For the earth has ever a home for a tender heart and
true !"

VII.

Even so it came to pass, as the angel promised then :

He wedded and wandered forth with the earliest friends
of Penn,

And the home foreshown he found, with all that a home
endears, —

A nest of plenty and peace, for a hundred and eighty
years !

VIII.

In beautiful Warwickshire the life of the two began, —

A slip of the tree of the dream, a far-off sire of the man ;

And it seemed to Gabriel Parke, as the leaves above him
stirred,

That the secret dream of his heart the soul of the holly
heard.

IX.

Of Patience Phillips he thought: she, too, was a bashful
maid :

The blue of her eyes was hid by the eyelash's golden
shade ;

But well that she could not hide the cheeks that were fair
to see

As the pink of an apple-bud, ere the blossom snows the
tree !

X.

Ah ! how had the English Parke to the English girl
betrayed,

Save a dream had helped his heart, the love that makes
afraid ? —

That seemed to smother his voice, when his blood so
  sweetly ran,
And the baby heart lay weak in the rugged breast of the
  man?

XI.

His glance came back from the hills and back from the
  laurel glen,
And fell on the grass at his feet, where clucked a mother-
  hen,
With a brood of tottering chicks, that followed as best
  they might;
But one was trodden and lame, and drooped in a woful
  plight.

XII.

He lifted up from the grass the feeble, chittering thing,
And warmed its breast at his lips, and smoothed its
  stumpy wing,
When, lo! at his side a voice: " Is it hurt?" was all she
  said;
But the eyes of both were shy, and the cheeks of both
  were red.

XIII.

She took from his hand the chick, and fondled and
  soothed it then,
While, knowing that good was meant, cheerfully clucked
  the hen ;
And the tongues of the two were loosed : there seemed a
  wonderful charm
In talk of the hatching fowls and spring-work done on the
  farm.

XIV.

But Gabriel saw that her eyes were drawn to the holly-
  tree :
" Have you heard," he said, " how it came with the family
  over the sea ? "
He told the story again, though he knew she knew it well,
And a spark of hope, as he spake, like fire in his bosom
  fell.

XV.

" I dreamed a beautiful dream, here, under the tree, just
  now,"
He said ; and Patience felt the warmth of his eyes on
  her brow :

" I dreamed, like the English Parke ; already the farm I
   own,
But the rest of the dream is best — the land is little,
   alone."

XVI.

He paused, and looked at the maid : her flushing cheek
   was bent,
And, under her chin, the chick was cheeping its warm
   content ;
But naught she answered — then he : "O Patience ! I
   thought of you !
Tell me you take the dream, and help me to make it
   true !"

XVII.

The mother looked from the house, concealed by the
   window-pane,
And she felt that the holly's spell had fallen upon the
   twain ;
She guessed from Gabriel's face what the words he had
   spoken were,
And blushed in the maiden's stead, as if they were spoken
   to her.

XVIII.

She blushed, and she turned away, ere the trembling man
and maid
Silently hand in hand had kissed in the holly's shade,
And Patience whispered at last, her sweet eyes dim with
dew :
" O Gabriel ! *could* you dream as much as I 've dreamed
of you ? "

XIX.

The mother said to herself, as she sat in her straight old
chair :
"He 's got the pick of the flock, so tidy and kind and fair!
At first I shall find it hard, to sit and be still, and see
How the house is kept to rights by somebody else than
me.

XX.

" But the home must be theirs alone : I 'll do by her, if I
can,
As Gabriel's grandmother did, when I as a wife began :
So good and faithful he 's been, from the hour when I
gave him life,
He shall master be in the house, and mistress shall be his
wife ! "

JOHN REED.

THERE 's a mist on the meadow below ; the herring-
frogs chirp and cry ;
It 's chill when the sun is down, and the sod is not yet
dry :
The world is a lonely place, it seems, and I don't know
why.

I see, as I lean on the fence, how wearily trudges Dan
With the feel of the spring in his bones, like a weak and
elderly man ;
I 've had it a many a time, but we must work when we
can.

But day after day to toil, and ever from sun to sun,
Though up to the season's front and nothing be left
undone,
Is ending at twelve like a clock, and beginning again at
one.

3 *

The frogs make a sorrowful noise, and yet it 's the time
  they mate ;
There 's something comes with the spring, a lightness or
  else a weight ;
There 's something comes with the spring, and it seems to
  me it 's fate.

It 's the hankering after a life that you never have learned
  to know ;
It 's the discontent with a life that is always thus and
  so ;
It 's the wondering what we are, and where we are going
  to go.

My life is lucky enough, I fancy, to most men's eyes,
For the more a family grows, the oftener some one dies,
And it 's now run on so long, it could n't be otherwise.

And Sister Jane and myself, we have learned to claim
  and yield ;
She rules in the house at will, and I in the barn and
  field,
So, nigh upon thirty years ! — as if written and signed
  and sealed.

I could n't change if I would ; I 've lost the how and the
  when ;

One day my time will be up, and Jane be the mistress
  then,

For single women are tough and live down the single
  men.

She kept me so to herself, she was always the stronger
  hand,

And my lot showed well enough, when I looked around
  in the land ;

But I 'm tired and sore at heart, and I don't quite
  understand.

I wonder how it had been if I 'd taken what others need,

The plague, they say, of a wife, the care of a younger
  breed ?

If Edith Pleasanton now were with me as Edith Reed ?

Suppose that a son well grown were there in the place
  of Dan,

And I felt myself in him, as I was when my work
  began ?

I should feel no older, sure, and certainly more a man !

A daughter, besides, in the house ; nay, let there be two
     or three !
We never can overdo the luck that can never be,
And what has come to the most might also have come
     to me.

I 've thought, when a neighbor's wife or his child was
     carried away,
That to have no loss was a gain ; but now, — I can
     hardly say ;
He seems to possess them still, under the ridges of clay.

And share and share in a life is, somehow, a different thing
From property held by deed, and the riches that oft take
     wing ;
I feel so close in the breast ! — I think it must be the
     spring.

I 'm drying up like a brook when the woods have been
     cleared around ;
You 're sure it must always run, you are used to the sight
     and sound,
But it shrinks till there 's only left a stony rut in the
     ground.

There 's nothing to do but take the days as they come
    and go,

And not to worry with thoughts that nobody likes to
    show,

For people so seldom talk of the things they want to
    know.

There 's times when the way is plain, and everything
    nearly right,

And then, of a sudden, you stand like a man with a
    clouded sight :

A bush seems often a beast, in the dusk of the falling
    night.

I must move ; my joints are stiff ; the weather is breed-
    ing rain,

And Dan is hurrying on with his plough-team up the lane.

I 'll go to the village-store ; I 'd rather not talk with Jane.

THE OLD PENNSYLVANIA FARMER.

I.

WELL — well! this is a comfort, now — the air is mild
    as May,
And yet 't is March the twentieth, or twenty-first, to-day :
And Reuben ploughs the hill for corn ; I thought it would
    be tough,
But now I see the furrows turned, I guess it 's dry enough.

II.

I don't half live, penned up in doors ; a stove 's not like
    the sun.
When I can't see how things go on, I fear they 're badly
    done :
I might have farmed till now, I think — one's family is
    so queer —
As if a man can't oversee who 's in his eightieth year !

III.

Father, I mind, was eighty-five before he gave up his ;
But he was dim o' sight, and crippled with the rheumatiz.
I followed in the old, steady way, so he was satisfied ;
But Reuben likes new-fangled things and ways I can't
    abide.

IV.

I'm glad I built this southern porch ; my chair seems
    easier here :
I have n't seen as fine a spring this five and twenty year !
And how the time goes round so quick ! — a week, I would
    have sworn,
Since they were husking on the flat, and now they plough
    for corn !

V.

When I was young, time had for me a lazy ox's pace,
But now it's like a blooded horse, that means to win the
    race.
And yet I can't fill out my days, I tire myself with
    naught ;
I'd rather use my legs and hands than plague my head
    with thought.

VI.

There 's Marshall, too, I see from here : he and his boys
   begin.
Why don't they take the lower field? that one is poor
   and thin.
A coat of lime it ought to have, but they 're a doless set :
They think swamp-mud 's as good, but we shall see what
   corn they get !

VII.

Across the level, Brown's new place begins to make a
   show ;
I thought he 'd have to wait for trees, but, bless me, how
   they grow !
They say it 's fine — two acres filled with evergreens and
   things ;
But so much land ! it worries me, for not a cent it
   brings.

VIII.

He has the right, I don't deny, to please himself that
   way,
But 't is a bad example set, and leads young folks astray :

Book-learning gets the upper-hand and work is slow and
    slack,

And they that come long after us will find things gone to
    wrack.

IX.

Now Reuben's on the hither side, his team comes back
    again ;

I know how deep he sets the share, I see the horses
    strain :

I had that field so clean of stones, but he must plough so
    deep,

He 'll have it like a turnpike soon, and scarcely fit for
    sheep.

X.

If father lived, I 'd like to know what he would say to
    these

New notions of the younger men, who farm by chem-
    istries :

There 's different stock and other grass ; there 's patent
    plough and cart —

Five hundred dollars for a bull ! it would have broke his
    heart.

XI.

The maples must be putting out: I see a something red

Down yonder where the clearing laps across the meadow's

head.

Swamp-cabbage grows beside the run ; the green is good

to see,

But wheat 's the color, after all, that cheers and 'livens

me.

XII.

They think I have an easy time, no need to worry now —

Sit in the porch all day and watch them mow, and sow,

and plough :

Sleep in the summer in the shade, in winter in the sun —

I 'd rather do the thing myself, and know just how it 's

done !

XIII.

Well — I suppose I 'm old, and yet 't is not so long ago

When Reuben spread the swath to dry, and Jesse learned

to mow,

And William raked, and Israel hoed, and Joseph pitched

with me :

But such a man as I was then my boys will never be !

XIV.

I don't mind William's hankering for lectures and for
    books ;
He never had a farming knack — you 'd see it in his
    looks ;
But handsome is that handsome does, and he is well to do :
'T would ease my mind if I could say the same of Jesse,
    too.

XV.

There 's one black sheep in every flock, so there must be
    in mine,
But I was wrong that second time his bond to undersign :
It 's less than what his share will be — but there 's the
    interest !
In ten years more I might have had two thousand to
    invest.

XVI.

There 's no use thinking of it now, and yet it makes me
    sore ;
The way I 've slaved and saved, I ought to count a little
    more.

I never lost a foot of land, and that 's a comfort, sure,
And if they do not call me rich, they cannot call me poor.

XVII.

Well, well! ten thousand times I 've thought the things
    I 'm thinking now ;
I 've thought them in the harvest-field and in the clover-
    mow ;
And often I get tired of them, and wish I 'd something
    new —
But this is all I 've had and known ; so what 's a man to
    do ?

XVIII.

'T is like my time is nearly out, of that I 'm not afraid ;
I never cheated any man, and all my debts are paid.
They call it rest that we shall have, but work would do no
    harm ;
There can't be rivers there, and fields, without some sort
    o' farm !

NAPOLEON AT GOTHA.

I.

WE walk amid the currents of actions left undone,
The germs of deeds that wither, before they see the sun.
For every sentence uttered, a million more are dumb:
Men's lives are chains of chances, and History their sum.

II.

Not he, the Syracusan, but each impurpled lord
Must eat his banquet under the hair-suspended sword ;
And one swift breath of silence may fix or change the fate
Of him whose force is building the fabric of a state.

III.

Where o'er the windy uplands the slated turrets shine,
Duke August ruled at Gotha, in Castle Friedenstein, —

A handsome prince and courtly, of light and shallow
  heart,
No better than he should be, but with a taste for Art.

IV.

The fight was fought at Jena, eclipsed was Prussia's sun,
And by the French invaders the land was overrun;
But while the German people were silent in despair,
Duke August painted pictures, and curled his yellow hair.

V.

Now, when at Erfurt gathered the ruling royal clan,
Themselves the humble subjects, their lord the Corsican,
Each bade to ball and banquet the sparer of his line:
Duke August with the others, to Castle Friedenstein.

VI.

Then were the larders rummaged, the forest-stags were
  slain,

The towers were bright with banners, — but all the
    people said :
" We, slaves, must feed our master, — would God that he
    were dead ! "

VII.

They drilled the ducal guardsmen, men young and
    straight and tall,
To form a double column, from gate to castle-wall ;
And as there were but fifty, the first must wheel away,
Fall in beyond the others, and lengthen the array.

VIII.

"*Parbleu!*" Napoleon muttered : " Your Highness' guards
    I prize,
So young and strong and handsome, and all of equal size!"
" You, Sire," replied Duke August, "may have as fine, if
    you
Will twice or thrice repeat them, as I am forced to do ! "

IX.

Now, in the Castle household, of all the folk, was one
Whose heart was hot within him, the Ducal Huntsman's
    son ;

A proud and bright-eyed stripling; scarce fifteen years he
　　had,
But free of hall and chamber: Duke August loved the lad.

X.

He saw the forceful homage; he heard the shouts that
　　came
From base throats, or unwilling, but equally of shame:
He thought: " *One* man has done it, — *one* life would free
　　the land,
But all are slaves and cowards, and none will lift a hand!

XI.

" My grandsire hugged a bear to death, when broke his
　　hunting-spear;
And has this little Frenchman a muzzle I should fear?
If kings are cowed, and princes, and all the land is scared,
Perhaps a boy can show them the thing they might have
　　dared! "

XII.

Napoleon on the morrow was coming once again,
(And all the castle knew it) without his courtly train;

And, when the stairs were mounted, there was no other
    road
But one long, lonely passage, to where the Duke abode.

XIII.

None guessed the secret purpose the silent stripling kept:
Deep in the night he waited, and, when his father slept,
Took from the rack of weapons a musket old and tried,
And cleaned the lock and barrel, and laid it at his side.

XIV.

He held it fast in slumber, he lifted it in dreams
Of sunlit mountain-forests and stainless mountain-streams;
And in the morn he loaded — the load was bullets three:
" For Deutschland — for Duke August — and now the
    third for me!"

XV.

" What! ever wilt be hunting?" the stately Marshal cried;
" I 'll fetch a stag of twenty!" the pale-faced boy replied,
As, clad in forest color, he sauntered through the court,
And said, when none could hear him: " Now, may the
    time be short!"

XVI.

The corridor was vacant, the windows full of sun ;
He stole within the midmost, and primed afresh his
    gun ;
Then stood, with all his senses alert in ear and eye
To catch the lightest signal that showed the Emperor
    nigh.

XVII.

A sound of wheels : a silence : the muffled sudden jar
Of guards their arms presenting : a footstep mounting
    far,
Then nearer, briskly nearer, — a footstep, and alone !
And at the farther portal appeared Napoleon !

XVIII.

Alone, his hands behind him, his firm and massive head
With brooded plans uplifted, he came with measured
    tread :
And yet, those feet had shaken the nations from their
    poise,
And yet, that will to shake them depended on the boy's !

XIX.

With finger on the trigger, the gun held hunter-wise,
His rapid heart-beats sending the blood to brain and
    eyes,
The boy stood, firm and deadly, — another moment's
    space,
And then the Emperor saw him, and halted, face to face.

XX.

A mouth as cut in marble, an eye that pierced and stung
As might a god's, all-seeing, the soul of one so young:
A look that read his secret, that lamed his callow will,
That inly smiled, and dared him his purpose to fulfil !

XXI.

As one a serpent trances, the boy, forgetting all,
Felt but that face, nor noted the harmless musket's
    fall ;
Nor breathed, nor thought, nor trembled ; but, pale and
    cold as stone,
Saw pass, nor look behind him, the calm Napoleon.

XXII.

And these two kept their secret; but from that day
     began
The sense of fate and duty that made the boy a man ;
And long he lived to tell it, — and, better, lived to say :
" God's purposes were grander : He thrust me from His
     way ! "

THE ACCOLADE.

I.

UNDER the lamp in the tavern yard
   The beggars and thieves were met ;
Ruins of lives that were evil-starred,
Battered bodies and faces hard,
   A loveless and lawless set.

II.

The cans were full, if the scrip was lean ;
   A fiddler played to the crowd
The high-pitched lilt of a tune obscene,
When there entered the gate, in garments mean,
   A stranger tall and proud.

III.

There was danger in their doubting eyes ;
   " Now who are you ? " they said.

" One who has been more wild than wise,
Who has played with force and fed on lies,
    As you on your mouldy bread.

IV.

" The false have come to me, high and low,
    Where I only sought the true :
I am sick of sham and sated with show ;
The honest evil I fain would know,
    In the license here with you."

V.

"He shall go!" " He shall stay!" In hot debate
    Their whims and humors ran,
When Jack o' the Strong Arm square and straight
Stood up, like a man whose word is fate,
    A reckless and resolute man.

VI.

" Why brawl," said he, " at so slight a thing?
    Are fifty afraid of one ?
We have taken a stranger into our ring
Ere this, and made him in sport our king ;
    So let it to-night be done !

VII.

" Fetch him a crown of tinsel bright,
  For sceptre a tough oak-staff ;
And who most serves to the King's delight,
The King shall dub him his own true knight,
  And I swear the King shall laugh ! "

VIII.

They brought him a monstrous tinsel crown,
  They put the staff in his hand ;
There was wrestling and racing up and down,
There was song of singer and jest of clown,
  There was strength and sleight-of-hand.

IX.

The King, he pledged them with clink of can,
  He laughed with a royal glee ;
There was dull mistrust when the sports began,
There was roaring mirth when the rearmost man
  Gave out, and the ring was free.

X.

For Jack o' the Strong Arm strove with a will,
  With the wit and the strength of four ;

There was never a part he dared not fill,
Wrestler, and singer, and clown, until
    The motley struggle was o'er.

XI.

And ever he turned from the deft surprise,
    And ever from strain or thrust,
With a dumb appeal in his laughing guise,
And gazéd on the King with wistful eyes,
    Panting, and rough with dust.

XII.

"Kneel, Jack o' the Strong Arm!   Our delight
    Hath most been due to thee,"
Said the King, and stretched his rapier bright:
" Rise, Sir John Armstrong, our true knight,
    Bold, fortunate, and free!"

XIII.

Jack o' the Strong Arm knelt and bowed,
    To meet the christening blade ;
He heard the shouts of the careless crowd,
And murmured something, as though he vowed,
    When he felt the accolade.

XIV.

He kissed the King's hand tenderly,
   Full slowly then did rise,
And within him a passion seemed to be ;
For his choking throat they all could see,
   And the strange tears in his eyes.

XV.

From his massive breast the rags he threw,
   He threw them from body and limb,
Till, bare as a new-born babe to view,
He faced them, no longer the man they knew :
   They silently stared at him.

XVI.

" O King ! " he said, " thou wert King, I knew ;
   I am verily knight, O King !
What thou hast done thou canst not undo ;
Thou hast come to the false and found the true
   In the carelessly ventúred thing.

XVII.

" As I cast away these rags I have worn,
   The life that was in them I cast ;

4 *   F

Take me, naked and newly born,

Test me with power and pride and scorn,

　　I shall be true to the last ! "

XVIII.

His large, clear eyes were weak as he spoke,

　　But his mouth was firm and strong ;

And a cry from the thieves and beggars broke,

As the King took off his own wide cloak

　　And covered him from the throng.

XIX.

He gave him his royal hand in their sight,

　　And he said, before the ring :

"Come with me, Sir John !　Be leal and right ;

If I have made thee all of a knight,

　　Thou hast made me more of a king ! "

ERIC AND AXEL.

I.

THOUGH they never divided my meat or wine,
Yet Eric and Axel are friends of mine ;
Never shared my sorrow, nor laughed with my glee,
Yet Eric and Axel are dear to me ;
And faithfuller comrades no man ever knew
Than Eric and Axel, the fearless, the true !

II.

When I hit the target, they feel no pride ;
When I spin with the waltzers, they wait outside ;
When the holly of Yule-tide hangs in the hall,
And kisses are freest, they care not at all ;
When I sing, they are silent ; I speak, they obey,
Eric and Axel, my hope and my stay !

III.

They wait for my coming; they know I shall come,

When the dancers are faint and the fiddlers numb,

With a shout of " Ho, Eric ! " and " Axel, ho ! "

As we skim the wastes of the Norrland snow,

And their frozen breath to a silvery gray

Turns Eric's raven and Axel's bay.

IV.

By the bondehus and the herregoard,

O'er the glassy pavement of frith and fiord,

Through the tall fir-woods, that like steel are drawn

On the broadening red of the rising dawn,

Till one low roof, where the hills unfold,

Shelters us all from the angry cold.

V.

I tell them the secret none else shall hear ;

I love her, Eric, I love my dear !

I love her, Axel ; wilt love her, too,

Though her eyes are dark and mine are blue ?

She has eyes like yours, so dark and clear :

Eric and Axel will love my dear ⊦

VI.

They would speak if they could ; but I think they know
Where, when the moon is thin, they shall go,
To wait awhile in the sleeping street,
To hasten away upon snow-shod feet, —
Away and away, ere the morning star
Touches the tops of the spires of Calmàr!

VII.

Per, the merchant, may lay at her feet
His Malaga wine and his raisins sweet,
Brought in his ships from Portugal land,
And I am as bare as the palm of my hand ;
But she sighs for me, and she sighs for you,
Eric and Axel, my comrades true !

VIII.

You care not, Eric, for gold and wine ;
You care not, Axel, for show and shine ;
But you care for the touch of the hand that 's dear,
And the voice that fondles you through the ear,
And you shall save us, through storm and snow,
When *she* calls : " Ho, Eric !" and " Axel, ho !"

LYRICS.

LYRICS.

———•———

THE BURDEN OF THE DAY.

I.

WHO shall rise and cast away,
First, the Burden of the Day?
Who assert his place, and teach
Lighter labor, nobler speech,
Standing firm, erect, and strong,
Proud as Freedom, free as Song?

II.

Lo! we groan beneath the weight
Our own weaknesses create;
Crook the knee and shut the lip,
All for tamer fellowship;
Load our slack, compliant clay
With the Burden of the Day!

III.

Higher paths there are to tread ;
Fresher fields around us spread ;
Other flames of sun and star
Flash at hand and lure afar ;
Larger manhood might we share,
Surer fortune, — did we dare !

IV.

In our mills of common thought
By the pattern all is wrought :
In our school of life, the man
Drills to suit the public plan,
And through labor, love, and play,
Shifts the Burden of the Day.

V.

Ah, the gods of wood and stone
Can a single saint dethrone,
But the people who shall aid
'Gainst the puppets they have made ?
First they teach and then obey :
'T is the Burden of the Day.

VI.

Thunder shall we never hear
In this ordered atmosphere?
Never this monotony feel
Shattered by a trumpet's peal?
Never airs that burst and blow
From eternal summits, know?

VII.

Though no man resent his wrong,
Still is free the poet's song :
Still, a stag, his thought may leap
O'er the herded swine and sheep,
And in pastures far away
Lose the Burden of the Day!

IN THE LISTS.

COULD I choose the age and fortunate season
   When to be born,
I would fly from the censure of your barren reason,
   And the scourges of your scorn :
Could I take the tongue, and the land, and the station
   That to me were fit,
I would make my life a force and an exultation,
   And you could not stifle it !

But the thing most near to the freedom I covet
   Is the freedom I wrest
From a time that would bar me from climbing above it,
   To seek the East in the West.
I have dreamed of the forms of a nobler existence
   Than you give me here,
And the beauty that lies afar in the dateless distance
   I would conquer, and bring more near.

It is good, undowered with the bounty of Fortune,
       In the sun to stand :
Let others excuse, and cringe, and importune,
       I will try the strength of my hand !
If I fail, I shall fall not among the mistaken,
       Whom you dare deride :
If I win, you shall hear, and see, and at last awaken
       To thank me because I defied !

THE SUNSHINE OF THE GODS.

I.

WHO shall sunder the fetters,
Who scale the invisible ramparts
Whereon our nimblest forces
Hurl their vigor in vain?
Where, like the baffling crystal
To a wildered bird of the heavens,
Something holds and imprisons
The eager, the stirring brain?

II.

Alas, from the fresh emotion,
From thought that is born of feeling,
From form, self-shaped, and slowly
Its own completeness evolving,
To the rhythmic speech, how long!

What hand shall master the tumult
Where one on the other tramples,
And none escapes a wrong?
Where the crowning germs of a thousand
Fancies encumber the portal,
Till one plucks a voice from the murmurs
And lifts himself into Song!

III.

As a man that walks in the mist,
As one that gropes for the morning
Through lengthening chambers of twilight,
The souls of the poems wander
Restless, and dumb, and lost,
Till the Word, like a beam of morning,
Shivers the pregnant silence,
And the light of speech descends
Like a tongue of the Pentecost!

IV.

Ah, moment not to be purchased,
Not to be won by prayers,

Not by toil to be conquered,

But given, lest one despair,

By the Gods in wayward kindness,

Stay — thou art all too fair !

Hour of the dancing measures,

Sylph of the dew and rainbow,

Let us clutch thy shining hair !

V.

For the mist is blown from the mind,

For the impotent yearning is over,

And the wings of the thoughts have power :

In the warmth and the glow creative

Existence mellows and ripens,

And a crowd of swift surprises

Sweetens the fortunate hour ;

Till a shudder of rapture loosens

The tears that hang on the eyelids

Like a breeze-suspended shower,

With a sense of heavenly freshness

Blown from beyond the sunshine,

And the blood, like the sap of the roses,

Breaks into bud and flower.

VI.

'T is the Sunshine of the Gods,
The sudden light that quickens,
Unites the nimble forces,
And yokes the shy expression
To the thoughts that waited long, —
Waiting and wooing vainly:
But now they meet like lovers
In the time of willing increase,
Each warming each, and giving
The kiss that maketh strong:
And the mind feels fairest May-time
In the marriage of its passions,
For Thought is one with Speech,
In the Sunshine of the Gods,
And Speech is one with Song!

VII.

Then a rhythmic pulse makes order
In the troops of wandering fancies:
Held in soft subordination,
Lo! they follow, lead, or fly.

5   G

The fields of their feet are endless,
And the heights and the deeps are open
To the glance of the equal sky:
And the Masters sit no longer
In inaccessible distance,
But give to the haughtiest question,
Smiling, a sweet reply.

VIII.

Dost mourn, because the moment
Is a gift beyond thy will, —
A gift thy dreams had promised,
Yet they gave to Chance its keeping
And fettered thy free achievement
With the hopes they not fulfil?
Dost sigh o'er the fleeting rapture,
The bliss of reconcilement
Of powers that work apart,
Yet lean on each other still?

IX.

Be glad, for this is the token,
The sign and the seal of the Poet:

Were it held by will or endeavor,
There were naught so precious in Song.
Wait: for the shadows unlifted
To a million that crave the sunshine,
Shall be lifted for thee erelong.
Light from the loftier regions
Here unattainable ever, —
Bath of brightness and beauty, —
Let it make thee glad and strong!
Not to clamor or fury,
Not to lament or yearning,
But to faith and patience cometh
The Sunshine of the Gods,
The hour of perfect Song!

NOTUS IGNOTO.

I.

Do you sigh for the power you dream of,
The fair, evasive secret,
The rare imagined passion,
O Friend unknown!
Do you haunt Egyptian portals,
Where, within, the laboring goddess
Yields to the hands of her chosen
The sacred child, alone?

II.

Ah, pause!   There is consolation
For you, and pride:
Free of choice and worship,
Spared the pang and effort,
Nor partial made by triumph,

The poet's limitations
You lightly set aside :
Revived, in your fresher spirit
The buds of my thought may blossom,
And the clew, from weary fingers
Fallen, become your guide !
The taker, even as the giver,
The user as the maker,
Soil as seed, and rain as sunshine,
Alike are glorified !

III.

Loss with gain is balanced ;
You may reach, when I but beckon ;
You may drink, though mine the vintage,
You complete what I begun.
When at the temple-door I falter,
You advance to the altar ;
I but rise to the daybreak,
You to the sun !
My goal is your beginning :
My steeps of aspiration
For you are won !

IV.

Hark ! the nightingale is chanting
As if her mate but knew ;
Yet the dream within me
Which the bird-voice wakens,
Takes from her unconscious
Prompting, form and hue :
So the song I sing you,
Voice alone of my being,
Song for the mate and the nestling,
Finer and sweeter meaning
May possess for you !
Lifting to starry summits,
Filling with infinite passion,
While the witless singer broodeth
In the darkness and the dew !

V.

Carved on the rock as an arrow
To point your path, am I :
A cloud that tells, in the heavens,
Which way the breezes fly :

A brook that is born in the meadows,
And wanders at will, nor guesses
Whither its waters hie :
A child that scatters blossoms,
Thoughtless of memoried odors
Or sweet surprises of color,
That waken when you go by :
A bee-bird of the woodland,
That finds the honeyed hollows
Of ancient oaks, for others, —
Even as these, am I !

VI.

Accept, and enjoy, and follow, —
Conquer wherein I yield !
Make yours the bright conclusion,
From me concealed !
Truth, to whom will possess it,
Beauty, to whom embraces,
Song and its inmost secret,
Life and its unheard music,
To whom will hear and know them,
Are ever revealed !

IN MY VINEYARD.

I.

AT last the dream that clad the field
　　Is fairest fact, and stable ;
At last my vines a covert yield,
　　A patch for song and fable.
I thread the rustling ranks, that hide
　　Their misty violet treasure,
And part the sprays with more than pride,
　　And more than owner's pleasure.

II.

The tender shoots, the fragrance fine,
　　Betray the garden's poet,
Whose daintiest life is turned to wine,
　　Yet half is shy to show it, —

The epicure, who yields to toil
    A scarce fulfilled reliance,
But takes from sun and dew and soil
    A grace unguessed by science.

III.

Faint odors, from the bunches blown,
    Surround me and subdue me ;
The vineyard-breath of many a zone
    Is softly breathing through me :
From slopes of Eshkol, in the sun,
    And many a hillside classic ;
From where Falernian juices run,
    And where they press the Massic !

IV.

Where airy terraces, on high,
    The hungry vats replenish,
And, less from earth than from the sky,
    Distil the golden Rhenish :
Where, light of heart, the Bordelais
    Compels his stony level
To burst and foam in purple spray, —
    The rose that crowns the revel !

5*

V.

So here, as there, the subject earth
    Shall take a tenderer duty ;
And Labor walk with harmless Mirth,
    And wed with loving Beauty :
So, here, a gracious life shall fix
    Its seat, in sunnier weather ;
For sap and blood so sweetly mix,
    And richly run together !

VI.

The vine was exiled from the land
    That bore but needful burdens ;
But now we slack the weary hand,
    And look for gentler guerdons :
We take from Ease a grace above
    The strength we took from Labor,
And win to laugh, and woo to love,
    Each grimly-earnest neighbor.

VII.

What idle dreams ! Even as I muse,
    I feel a falling shadow ;

And vapors blur and clouds confuse
    My coming Eldorado.
Portentous, grim, a ghost draws nigh,
    To clip my flying fancy,
And change the shows of earth and sky
    With evil necromancy.

VIII.

The leaves on every vine-branch curl
    As if a frost had stung them ;
The bunches shrivel, snap, and whirl
    As if a tempest flung them ;
And as the ghost his forehead shakes,
    Denying and commanding,
But withered stalks and barren stakes
    Surround me where I 'm standing.

IX.

" Beware ! " the spectre cried ; " the woe
    Of this delusive culture !
The nightingale that lures thee so
    Shall hatch a ravening vulture.

To feed the vat, to fill the bin,

    Thou pluck'st the vineyard's foison,

That drugs the cup of mirth with sin,

    The veins of health with poison ! "

         X.

But now a golden mist was born,

    With violet odors mingled :

I felt a brightness, as of morn,

    And all my pulses tingled ;

And forms arose, — among them first

    The old Ionian lion,

And they, Sicilian Muses nursed, —

    Theocritus and Bion.

         XI.

And he of Teos, he of Rome,

    The Sabine bard and urban ;

And Saadi, from his Persian home,

    And Hafiz in his turban :

And Shakespeare, silent, sweet, and grave,

    And Herrick with his lawns on ;

And Luther, mellow, burly, brave,

    Along with Rare Ben Jonson !

XII.

"Be comforted!" they seemed to say;
    "For Nature does no treasons:
She neither gives nor takes away
    Without eternal reasons.
She heaps the stores of corn and oil
    In such a liberal measure,
That, past the utmost need of Toil,
    There 's something left for Pleasure.

XIII.

"The secret soul of sun and dew
    Not vainly she distilleth,
And from these globes of pink and blue
    A harmless cup she filleth:
Who loveth her may take delight
    In what for him she dresses,
Nor find in cheerful appetite
    The portal to excesses.

XIV.

"Yes, ever since the race began
    To press the vineyard's juices,

It was the brute within the man
    Defiled their nobler uses ;
But they who take from order joy,
    And make denial duty,
Provoke the brute they should destroy
    By Freedom and by Beauty ! "

XV.

They spake ; and, lo ! the baleful shape
    Grew dim, and then retreated ;
And bending o'er the hoarded grape,
    The vines my vision greeted.
The sunshine burst, the breezes turned
    The leaves till they were hoary,
And over all the vineyard burned
    A fresher light of glory !

THE TWO HOMES.

I.

My home was seated high and fair,
  Upon a mountain's side ;
The day was longest, brightest there ;
  Beneath, the world was wide.
Across its blue, embracing zone
The rivers gleamed, the cities shone,
And over the edge of the fading rim
I saw the storms in the distance dim,
  And the flash of the soundless thunder.

II.

But weary grew the sharp, cold wine
  Of winds that never kissed,
The changeless green of fir and pine,
  The gray and clinging mist.

Above the granite sprang no bowers ;
The soil gave low and scentless flowers ;
And the drone and din of the waterfall
Became a challenge, a taunting call :
    " 'T is fair, 't is fair in the valley ! "

III.

Of all the homesteads deep and far
    My fancy clung to one,
Whose gable burned, a mellow star,
    Touched by the sinking sun.
Unseen around, but not unguessed,
The orchards made a leafy nest ;
The turf before it was thick, I knew,
And bees were busy the garden through.
    And the windows were dark with roses.

IV.

" 'T is happier there, below," I sighed :
    The world is warm and near,
And closer love and comfort hide.
    That cannot reach me here.

Who there abides must be so blest
He 'll share with me his sheltered nest,
If down to the valley I should go,
Leaving the granite, the pines and snow,
    And the winds that are keen as lances."   ·

V.

I wandered down, by ridge and dell ;
    The way was rough and long :
Though earlier shadows round me fell,
    I cheered them with my song.
The world's great circle narrower grew,
Till hedge and thicket hid the blue ;
But over the orchards, near at hand,
The gable shone on the quiet land,
    And far away was the mountain !

VI.

Then came the master : mournful-eyed
    And stern of brow was he.
"O, planted in such peace !" I cried,
    "Spare but the least to me !"

"Who seeks," he said, "this brooding haze,
The tameness of these weary days?
The highway's dust, the glimmer and heat,
The woods that fetter the young wind's feet,
   And hide the world and its beauty?"

VII.

He stretched his hand ; he looked afar
   With eyes of old desire :
I saw my home, a mellow star
   That held the sunset's fire.
" But yonder home," he cried, " how fair !
Its chambers burn like gilded air ;
I know that the gardens are wild as dreams,
With the sweep of winds, the dash of streams,
   And the pines that sound as an anthem !

VIII.

" So quiet, so serenely high
   It sits, when clouds are furled,
And knows the beauty of the sky,
   The glory of the world !

Who there abides must be so blest
He 'll share with me that lofty crest,
If up to the mountain I should go,
Leaving the dust and the glare below,
  And the weary life of the valley!"

IRIS.

I.

I AM born from the womb of the cloud
  And the strength of the ardent sun,
When the winds have ceased to be loud,
  And the rivers of rain to run.
Then light, on my sevenfold arch,
  I swing in the silence of air,
While the vapors beneath me march
  And leave the sweet earth bare.

II.

For a moment, I hover and gleam
  On the skirts of the sinking storm ;
And I die in the bliss of the beam
  That gave me being and form.

I fade, as in human hearts
    The rapture that mocks the will:
I pass, as a dream departs
    That cannot itself fulfil!

III.

Beyond the bridge I have spanned
    The fields of the Poet unfold,
And the riches of Fairyland
    At my bases of misty gold.
I keep the wealth of the spheres
    Which the high Gods never have won;
And I coin, from their airy tears,
    The diadem of the sun!

IV.

For some have stolen the grace
    That is hidden in rest or strife;
And some have copied the face
    Or echoed the voice of Life;
And some have woven of sound
    A chain of the sweetest control,

And some have fabled or found
   The key to the human soul:

V.

But I, from the blank of the air
   And the white of the barren beam,
Have wrought the colors that flare
   In the forms of a painter's dream.
I gather the souls of the flowers,
   And the sparks of the gems, to me;
Till pale are the blossoming bowers,
   And dim the chameleon sea!

VI.

By the soul's bright sun, the eye,
   I am thrown on the artist's brain;
He follows me, and I fly;
   He pauses, I stand again.
O'er the reach of the painted world
   My chorded colors I hold,
On a canvas of cloud impearled
   Drawn with a brush of gold!

VII.

If I lure, as a mocking sprite,
　I give, as a goddess bestows,
The red, with its soul of might,
　And the blue, with its cool repose ;
The yellow that beckons and beams,
　And the gentler children they bear :
For the portal of Art's high dreams
　Is builded of Light and Air !

IMPLORA PACE.

THE clouds that stoop from yonder sky
  Discharge their burdens, and are free ;
The streams that take them hasten by,
  To find relief in lake and sea.

The wildest wind in vales afar
  Sleeps, pillowed on its ruffled wings ;
And song, through many a stormy bar,
  Beats into silence on the strings !

And love o'ercomes his young unrest,
  And first ambition's flight is o'er ;
And doubt is cradled on the breast
  Of perfect faith, and speaks no more.

Our dreams and passions cease to dare,
  And homely patience learns her part ;
Yet still some keen, pursuing care
  Forbids content to brain and heart.

The gift unreached, beyond the hand;
   The fault in all of beauty won;
The mildew of the harvest land,
   The spots upon the risen sun!

And still some cheaper service claims
   The will that leaps to loftier call:
Some cloud is cast on splendid aims,
   On power achieved some common thrall.

To spoil each beckoning victory,
   A thousand pygmy hands are thrust;
And, round each height attained, we see
   Our ether dim with lower dust.

Ah, could we breathe some peaceful air,
   And all save purpose there forget,
Till eager courage learn to bear
   The gadfly's sting, the pebble's fret!

Let higher goal and harsher way,
   To test our virtue, then combine!
'T is not for idle ease we pray,
   But freedom for our task divine.

6

PENN CALVIN.

I.

SEARCH high and low, search up and down,
    By light of stars or sun,
And of all the good folks of our town
    There 's like Penn Calvin none.
He lightly laughs when all condemn,
    He smiles when others pray ;
And what is sorest truth to them
    To him is idle play.

II.

" Penn Calvin, lift, as duty bids,
    The load we all must bear ! "
He only lifts his languid lids,
    And says : " The morn is fair ! "

" Learn while you may ! for Life is stern,
   And Art, alas ! is long."
He hums and answers : " Yes, I learn
   The cadence of a song."

III.

" The world is dark with human woe ;
   Man eats of bitter food."
" The world," he says, " is all aglow
   With beauty, bliss, and good ! "
" To crush the senses you must strive,
   The beast of flesh destroy ! "
" God gave this body, all alive,
   And every sense is joy ! "

IV.

" Nay, these be heathen words we hear ;
   The faith they teach is flown, —
A mist that clings to temples drear
   And altars overthrown."
" I reck not how nor whence it came,"
   He answers ; " I possess :

If heathens felt and owned the same,
    How bright was heathenesse ! "

V.

" Though you be stubborn to believe,
    Yet learn to grasp and hold :
There 's power and honor to achieve,
    And royal rule of gold ! "
Penn Calvin plucked an open rose
    And carolled to the sky :
" Shine, sun of Day, until its close, —
    They live, and so do I ! "

VI.

His eyes are clear as they were kissed
    By some unrisen dawn ;
Our grave and stern philanthropist
    Looks sad, and passes on.
Our pastor scowls ; the pious flock
    Avert their heads, and flee ;
For pestilence or earthquake-shock
    Less dreadful seems than he.

But all the children round him cling,
    Depraved as they were born ;
And vicious men his praises sing,
    Whom he forgets to scorn.
Penn Calvin's strange indifference gives
    Our folks a grievous care :
He 's simply glad because he lives,
    And glad the world is fair !

SUMMER NIGHT.

VARIATIONS ON CERTAIN MELODIES.

I.

ANDANTE.

UNDER the full-blown linden and the plane,
That link their arms above
In mute, mysterious love,
I hear the strain !
Is it the far postilion's horn,
Mellowed by starlight, floating up the valley,
Or song of love-sick peasant, borne
Across the fields of fragrant corn,
And poplar-guarded alley?
Now from the woodbine and the unseen rose
What new delight is showered ?
The warm wings of the air
Drop into downy indolence and close,
So sweetly overpowered :
But nothing sleeps, though rest seems everywhere.

II.

ADAGIO.

Something came with the falling dusk,
　　Came, and quickened to soft unrest :
Something floats in the linden's musk,
　　And throbs in the brook on the meadow's breast.
Shy Spirit of Love, awake, awake !
　　　　All things feel thee,
　　　　And all reveal thee :
　　The night was given for thy sweet sake.
Toil slinks aside, and leaves to thee the land ;
The heart beats warmer for the idle hand ;
　　　The timid tongue unlearns its wrong,
　　　　And speech is turned to song ;
　　　　The shaded eyes are braver ;
And every life, like flowers whose scent is dumb
　　　　Till dew and darkness come,
　　　　Gives forth a tender savor.
　　O, each so lost in all, who may resist
　　　　The plea of lips unkissed,
　　　　Or, hearing such a strain,
Though kissed a thousand times, kiss not again !

III.

APPASSIONATO.

Was it a distant flute
That breathed, and now is mute?
Or that lost soul men call the nightingale,
In bosky coverts hidden,
Filling with sudden passion all the vale?
O, chant again the tale,
And call on her whose name returns, unbidden,
A longing and a dream,
Adelaïda!
For while the sprinkled stars
Sparkle, and wink, and gleam,
Adelaïda!
Darkness and perfume cleave the unknown bars
Between the enamored heart and thee,
And thou and I are free,
Adelaïda!
Less than a name, a melody, art thou,
A hope, a haunting vow!
The passion-cloven
Spirit of thy Beethoven

Claimed with less ardor than I claim thee now,
        Adelaïda!
Take form, at last : from these o'erbending branches
      Descend, or from the grass arise !
        I scarce shall see thine eyes,
      Or know what blush the shadow stanches ;
But all my being's empty urn shall be
        Filled with thy mystery !

IV.

CAPRICCIOSO.

      Nay, nay ! the longings tender,
    The fear, the marvel, and the mystery,
The shy, delicious dread, the unreserved surrender,
      Give, if thou canst, to me !
        For I would be,
      In this expressive languor,
While night conceals, the wooed and not the wooer ;
Shaken with supplication, keen as anger ;
      Pursued, and thou pursuer !
Plunder my bosom of its hoarded fire,   ·
      And so assail me,
     That coy denial fail me,

6*   I

Slain by the mirrored shape of my desire !

       Though life seem overladen

With conquered bliss, it only craves the more :

Teach me the other half of passion's lore —

     Be thou the man, and I the maiden !

         Ah ! come,

    While earth is waiting, heaven is dumb,

      And blossom-sighs

   So penetrate the indolent air,

The very stars grow fragrant in the skies !

        Arise,

    And thine approach shall make me fair,

Thy borrowed pleading all too soon subdue me,

     Till both forget the part ;

     And she who failed to woo me,

So caught, is held to my impatient heart !

THE SLEEPER.

THE glen was fair as some Arcadian dell,
   All shadow, coolness, and the rush of streams,
Save where the sprinkled blaze of noonday fell
   Like stars within its under-sky of dreams.
Rich leaf and blossomed grape and fern-tuft made
Odors of life and slumber through the shade.

"O peaceful heart of Nature!" was my sigh ;
   " How dost thou shame, in thine unconscious bliss,
Thy sure accordance with the changing sky,
   O quiet heart, the restless beat of this!
Take thou the place false friends have vacant left,
And bring thy bounty to repair the theft!"

So sighing, weary with the unsoothed pain
   From insect-stings of women and of men,

Uneasy heart and ever-baffled brain,
   I breathed the lonely beauty of the glen,
And from the fragrant shadows where she stood
Evoked the shyest Dryad of the wood.

Lo! on a slanting rock, outstretched at length,
   A woodman lay in slumber, fair as death,
His limbs relaxed in all their supple strength,
   His lips half parted with his easy breath,
And by one gleam of hovering light caressed
His bare brown arm and white uncovered breast.

"Why comes he here?" I whispered, treading soft
   The hushing moss beside his flinty bed;
"Sweet are the haycocks in yon clover-croft,—
   The meadow turf were light beneath his head:
Could he not slumber by the orchard-tree,
And leave this quiet unprofaned for me?"

But something held my step.   I bent, and scanned
   (As one might view a veiny agate-stone)
The hard, half-open fingers of his hand,
   Strong cords of wrist, knit round the jointed bone,

And sunburnt muscles, firm and full of power,
But harmless now as petals of a flower.

There lay the unconscious Life, but, ah! more fair
   Than ever blindly stirred in leaf and bark, —
Warmth, beauty, passion, mystery everywhere,
   Beyond the Dryad's feebly burning spark
Of cold poetic being: who could say
If here the angel or the wild beast lay?

Then I looked up, and read his helpless face:
   Peace touched the temples and the eyelids, slept
On drooping lashes, made itself a place
   In smiles that slowly to the corners crept
Of parting lips, and came and went, to show
The happy freedom of the heart below.

A holy rest! wherein the man became
   Man's interceding representative:
In Sleep's white realm fell off his mask of blame,
   And he was sacred, for that he did live.
His presence marred no more the quiet deep,
But all the glen became a shrine of Sleep!

And then I mused : how lovely this repose !

    How the shut sense its dwelling consecrates !

Sleep guards itself against the hands of foes ;

    Its breath disarms the Envies and the Hates

Which haunt our lives : were this mine enemy,

My stealthy watch could not less reverent be !

So hang their hands, that would have done me wrong ;

    So sweet their breathing, whose unkindly spite

Provoked the bitter measures of my song ;

    So might they slumber, sacred in my sight,

Or I in theirs : — why waste contentious breath ?

Forget, like Sleep ; and then forgive, like Death !

MY FARM: A FABLE.

WITHIN a green and pleasant land
 I own a favorite plantation,
Whose woods and meads, if rudely planned,
 Are still, at least, my own creation.
   Some genial sun or kindly shower
   Has here and there wooed forth a flower,
And touched the fields with expectation.

I know what feeds the soil I till,
 What harvest-growth it best produces:
My forests shape themselves at will,
 My grapes mature their proper juices.
   I know the brambles and the weeds,
   But know the fruits and wholesome seeds, —
Of those the hurt, of these the uses.

And working early, working late,
   Directing crude and random Nature,
'T is joy to see my small estate
   Grow fairer in the slightest feature.
      If but a single w.ld-rose blow,
      Or fruit-tree bend with April snow,
   That day am I the happiest creature!

But round the borders of the land
   Dwell many neighbors, fond of roving ;
With curious eye and prying hand
   About my fields I see them moving.
      Some tread my choicest herbage down,
      And some of weeds would weave a crown,
   And bid me wear it, unreproving.

"What trees!" says one ; "who ever saw
   A grove, like this, of *my* possessing?
This vale offends my upland's law ;
   This sheltered garden needs suppressing.
      My rocks this grass would never yield,
      And how absurd the level field!
   What here will grow is past my guessing."

" Behold the slope ! " another cries :
   " No sign of bog or meadow near it !
A varied surface I despise :
   There 's not a stagnant pool to cheer it ! "
      " Why plough at all ? " remarked a third.
      " Heaven help the man ! " a fourth I heard, —
   " His farm 's a jungle : let him clear it ! "

No friendly counsel I disdain :
   My fields are free to every comer ;
Yet that which one to praise is fain
   But makes another's visage glummer.
      I bow them out, and welcome in,
      But while I seek some truth to win
   Goes by, unused, the golden summer !

Ah ! vain the hope to find in each
   The wisdom each denies the other ;
These mazes of conflicting speech
   All theories of culture smother.
      I 'll raise and reap, with honest hand,
      The native harvest of my land ;
   Do thou the same, my wiser brother !

HARPOCRATES.

"The rest is silence." — HAMLET.

I.

THE message of the god I seek
   In voice, in vision, or in dream,
Alike on frosty Dorian peak,
   Or by the slow Arcadian stream :
Where'er the oracle is heard,
   I bow the head and bend the knee ;
In dream, in vision, or in word,
   The sacred secret reaches me.

II.

Athwart the dim Trophonian caves,
   Bat-like, the gloomy whisper flew ;
The lisping plash of Paphian waves
   Bathed every pulse in fiery dew :

From Phœbus, on his cloven hill,
　A shaft of beauty pierced the air,
And oaks of gray Dodona still
　Betrayed the Thunderer's presence there.

III.

The warmth of love, the grace of art,
　The joys that breath and blood express,
The desperate forays of the heart
　Into an unknown wilderness, —
All these I know : but sterner needs
　Demand the knowledge which must dower
The life that on achievement feeds,
　The grand activity of power.

IV.

What each reveals the shadow throws
　Of something unrevealed behind ;
The Secret's lips forever close
　To mock the secret undivined :
Thence late I come, from weary dreams
　The son of Isis to implore,
Whose temple-front of granite gleams
　Across the Desert's yellow floor.

V.

Lo ! where the sand, insatiate, drinks
   The steady splendor of the air,
Crouched on her heavy paws, the Sphinx
   Looks forth with old, unwearied stare !
Behind her, on the burning wall,
   The long processions flash and glow :
The pillared shadows of the hall
   Sleep with their lotus-crowns below.

VI.

A square of dark beyond, the door
   Breathes out the deep adytum's gloom :
I cross the court's deserted floor,
   And stand within the sacred room.
The priests repose from finished rite ;
   No echo rings from pavements trod ;
And sits alone, in swarthy light,
   The naked child, the temple's god.

VII.

No sceptre, orb, or mystic toy
   Proclaims his godship, young and warm

He sits alone, a naked boy,
　Clad in the beauty of his form.
Dark, solemn stars, of radiance mild,
　His eyes illume the golden shade,
And sweetest lips that never smiled
　The finger hushes, on them laid.

VIII.

O, never yet in trance or dream
　That falls when crowned desire has died,
So breathed the air of power supreme,
　So breathed, and calmed, and satisfied !
Those mystic lips were not unsealed
　The temple's awful hush to break,
But unto inmost sense revealed,
　The deity his message spake :

IX.

" If me thou knowest, stretch thy hand
　And my possessions thou shalt reach :
I grant no help, I break no band,
　I sit above the gods that teach.
The latest born, my realm includes
　The old, the strong, the near, the far, —

Serene beyond their changeful moods,
   And fixed as Night's unmoving star.

X.

" A child, I leave the dance of Earth
   To be my hornéd mother's care :
My father Ammon's Bacchic mirth,
   Delighting gods, I may not share.
I turn from Beauty, Love, and Power,
   In singing vale, on laughing sea ;
From Youth and Hope, and wait the hour
   When weary Knowledge turns to me.

XI.

" Beneath my hand the sacred springs
   Of Man's mysterious being burst,
And Death within my shadow brings
   The last of life, to greet the first.
There is no god, or grand or fair,
   On Orean or Olympian field,
But must to me his treasures bear,
   His one peculiar secret yield.

XII.

" I wear no garment, drop no shade
   Before the eyes that all things see ;
My worshippers, howe'er arrayed,
   Come in their nakedness to me.
The forms of life like gilded towers
   May soar, in air and sunshine drest, —
The home of Passions and of Powers, —
   Yet mine the crypts whereon they rest.

XIII.

" Embracing all, sustaining all,
   Consoling with unuttered lore,
Who finds me in my voiceless hall
   Shall need the oracles no more.
I am the knowledge that insures
   Peace, after Thought's bewildering range ;
I am the patience that endures ;
   I am the truth that cannot change ! "

RUN WILD.

HERE was the gate.   The broken paling,
   As if before the wind, inclines,
The posts half rotted, and the pickets, failing,
      Held only up by vines.

The plum-trees stand, though gnarled and speckled
   With leprosy of old disease ;
By cells of wormy life the trunks are freckled,
      And moss enfolds their knees.

I push aside the boughs and enter :
   Alas ! the garden's nymph has fled,
With every charm that leaf and blossom lent her,
      And left a hag instead.

Some female satyr from the thicket,
   Child of the bramble and the weed,
Sprang shouting over the unguarded wicket
     With all her savage breed.

She banished hence the ordered graces
   That smoothed a way for Beauty's feet,
And gave her ugliest imps the vacant places,
     To spoil what once was sweet.

Here, under rankling mulleins, dwindle
   The borders, hidden long ago ;
Here shoots the dock in many a rusty spindle,
     And purslane creeps below.

The thyme runs wild, and vainly sweetens,
   Hid from its bees, the conquering grass ;
And even the rose with briery menace threatens
     To tear me as I pass.

Where show the weeds a grayer color,
   The stalks of lavender and rue
Stretch like imploring arms, — but, ever duller,
     They slowly perish too.

Only the pear-tree's fruitless scion
    Exults above the garden's fall ;
Only the thick-maned ivy, like a lion,
        Devours the crumbling wall.

What still survives becomes as savage
    As that which entered to destroy,
Taking an air of riot and of ravage,
        Of strange and wanton joy.

No copse unpruned, no mountain hollow,
    So lawless in its growth may be :
Where the wild weeds have room to chase and follow,
        They graceful are, and free.

But Nature here attempts revenges
    For her obedience unto toil ;
She brings her rankest life with loathsome changes
        To smite the fattened soil.

For herbs of sweet and wholesome savor
    She plants her stems of bitter juice ;
From flowers she steals the scent, from fruits the flavor
        From homelier things the use.

Her angel is a mocking devil,
    If once the law relax its bands ;
In Man's neglected fields she holds her revel,
        Takes back, and spoils his lands.

Once having broken ground, he never
    The virgin sod can plant again :
The soil demands his services forever, —
        And God gives sun and rain !

"CASA GUIDI WINDOWS."

RETURNED to warm existence, — even as one
Sentenced, then blotted from the headsman's book,
Accepts with doubt the life again begun, —
I leave the duress of my couch, and look
Through Casa Guidi windows to the sun.

A fate like Farinata's held me fast
In some devouring pit of fever-fire,
Until, from ceaseless forms of toil that cast
Their will upon me, whirled in endless gyre,
The Spirit of the House brought help at last.

With Giotto wrestling, through the desperate hours
A thousand crowded frescos must I paint,
Or snatch from twilights dim, and dusky bowers,
Alternate forms of bacchanal and saint,
The streets of Florence and her beauteous towers.

Weak, wasted with those torments of the brain,
The circles of the Tuscan master's hell
Were dreams no more ; but when their fiery strain
Was fiercest, deep and sudden stillness fell
Athwart the storm, and all was peace again.

She came, whom Casa Guidi's chambers knew,
And know more proudly, an Immortal, now ; .
The air without a star was shivered through
With the resistless radiance of her brow,
And glimmering landscapes from the darkness grew.

Thin, phantom like ; and yet she brought me rest.
Unspoken words, an understood command
Sealed weary lids with sleep, together pressed
In clasping quiet wandering hand to hand,
And smoothed the folded cloth above the breast.

Now, looking through these windows, where the day
Shines on a terrace splendid with the gold
Of autumn shrubs, and green with glossy bay,
Once more her face, re-made from dust, I hold
In light so clear it cannot pass away : —

The quiet brow ; the face so frail and fair
For such a voice of song ; the steady eye,
Where shone the spirit fated to outwear
Its fragile house ; — and on her features lie
The soft half-shadows of her drooping hair.

Who could forget those features, having known ?
Whose memory do his kindling reverence wrong
That heard the soft Ionian flute, whose tone
Changed with the silver trumpet of her song ?
No sweeter airs from woman's lips were blown.

Ah, in the silence she has left behind
How many a sorrowing voice of life is still !
Songless she left the land that cannot find
Song for its heroes ; and the Roman hill,
Once free, shall for her ghost the laurel wind.

The tablet tells you, " Here she wrote and died,"
And grateful Florence bids the record stand :
Here bend Italian love and English pride
Above her grave, — and one remoter land,
Free as her prayers would make it, at their side.

I will not doubt the vision : yonder see
The moving clouds that speak of freedom won !
And life, new-lighted, with a lark-like glee
Through Casa Guidi windows hails the sun,
Grown from the rest her spirit gave to me.

FLORENCE, 1867.

THE GUESTS OF NIGHT.

I RIDE in a gloomy land,
   I travel a ghostly shore, —
Shadows on either hand,
   Darkness behind and before ;
Veils of the summer night
   Dusking the woods I know ;
A whisper haunts the height,
   And the rivulet croons below.

A waft from the roadside bank
   Tells where the wild-rose nods ;
The hollows are heavy and dank
   With the steam of the golden-rods :
Incense of Night and Death,
   Odors of Life and Day,
Meet and mix in a breath,
   Drug me, and lapse away.

Is it the hand of the Past,
  Stretched from its open tomb,
Or a spell from thy glamoury cast,
  O mellow and mystic gloom?
All, wherein I have part,
  All that was loss or gain,
Slips from the clasping heart,
  Breaks from the grasping brain.

Lo, what is left? I am bare
  As a new-born soul, — I am naught ;
My deeds are as dust in air,
  My words are as ghosts of thought.
I ride through the night alone,
  Detached from the life that seemed,
And the best I have felt or known
  Is less than the least I dreamed.

But the Night, like Agrippa's glass,
  Now, as I question it, clears ;
Over its vacancy pass
  The shapes of the crowded years ;

7 *

Meanest and most august,
  Hated or loved, I see
The dead that have long been dust,
  The living, so dead to me!

Place in the world's applause?
  Nay, there is nothing there!
Strength from unyielding laws?
  A gleam, and the glass is bare.
The lines of a life in song?
  Faint runes on the rocks of time?
I see but a formless throng
  Of shadows that fall or climb.

What else?   Am I then despoiled
  Of the garments I wove and wore?
Have I so refrained and toiled,
  To find there is naught in store?
I have loved, — I love!   Behold,
  How the steady pictures rise!
And the shadows are pierced with gold
  From the stars of immortal eyes.

Nearest or most remote,
  But dearest, hath none delayed ;
And the spirits of kisses float
  O'er the lips that never fade.
The Night each guest denies
  Of the hand or haughty brain,
But the loves that were, arise,
  And the loves that are, remain.

CHANT.

FOR THE BRYANT FESTIVAL.

November 5, 1864.

ONE hour be silent, sounds of war !
  Delay the battle he foretold,
And let the Bard's triumphant star
  Send down from heaven its milder gold !

Let Fame, that plucks but laurel now
  For loyal heroes, turn away,
And twine, to crown our poet's brow,
  The greener garland of the bay.

For he, our earliest minstrel, fills
  The land with echoes, sweet and long,
Gives language to her silent hills,
  And bids her rivers move to song.

The Phosphor of the Nation's dawn,
  Sole-risen above our tuneless coast,
As Hesper, now, his lamp burns on, —
  The leader of the starry host.

He sings of mountains and of streams,
  Of storied field and haunted dale,
Yet hears a voice through all his dreams,
  Which says: "The Good shall yet prevail."

He sings of Truth, he sings of Right ;
  He sings of Freedom, and his strains
March with our armies to the fight,
  Ring in the bondman's falling chains.

God, bid him live, till in her place
  Truth, crushed to earth, again shall rise, —
The "mother of a mighty race"
  Fulfil her poet's prophecies !

IMPROVISATIONS.

I.

THROUGH the lonely halls of the night
    My fancies fly to thee:
Through the lonely halls of the night,
    Alone, I cry to thee.
    For the stars bring presages
Of love, and of love's delight:
    Let them bear my messages
Through the lonely halls of the night!

In the golden porch of the morn
    Thou com'st anew to me:
In the golden porch of the morn,
    Say, art thou true to me?
    If dreams have shaken thee
With the call thou canst not scorn,
    Let Love awaken thee
In the golden porch of the morn!

II.

The rose of your cheek is precious ;
    Your eyes are warmer than wine ;
You catch men's souls in the meshes
    Of curls that ripple and shine —
        But, ah ! not mine.

Your lips are a sweet persuasion ;
    Your bosom a sleeping sea ;
Your voice, with its fond evasion,
    Is a call and a charm to me ;
        But I am free !

As the white moon lifts the waters,
    You lift the passions, and lead ;
As a chieftainess proud with slaughters,
    You smile on the hearts that bleed :
        But I take heed !

III.

Come to me, Lalage !
Girl of the flying feet,

Girl of the tossing hair
And the red mouth, small and sweet ;
Less of the earth than air,
So witchingly fond and fair,
Lalage !   .

Touch me, Lalage !
Girl of the soft white hand,
Girl of the low white brow
And the roseate bosom band ;
Bloom from an orchard bough
Less downy-soft than thou,
Lalage !

Kiss me, Lalage !
Girl of the fragrant breath,
Girl of the sun of May ;
As a bird that flutters in death,
My fluttering pulses say :
If thou be Death, yet stay,
Lalage !

IV.

What if I couch in the grass, or listlessly rock on the
   waters?

If in the market I stroll, sit by the beakers of wine?

Witched by the fold of a cloud, the flush of a meadow in
   blossom,

Soothed by the amorous airs, touched by the lips of the
   dew?

First must be color and odor, the simple, unmingled
   sensation,

Then, at the end of the year, apples and honey and grain.

You, reversing the order, your barren and withering
   branches

Vainly will shake in the winds, mine hanging heavy with
   gold!

V.

Though thy constant love I share,
   Yet its gift is rarer;
In my youth I thought thee fair;
   Thou art older and fairer!

K

Full of more than young delight
    Now day and night are ;
For the presence, then so bright,
    Is closer, brighter.

In the haste of youth we miss
    Its best of blisses :
Sweeter than the stolen kiss
    Are the granted kisses.

Dearer than the words that hide
    The love abiding,
Are the words that fondly chide,
    When love needs chiding.

Higher than the perfect song
    For which love longeth,
Is the tender fear of wrong,
    That never wrongeth.

She whom youth alone makes dear
    May awhile seem nearer :
Thou art mine so many a year,
    The older, the dearer !

VI.

A grass-blade is my warlike lance,
   A rose-leaf is my shield ;
Beams of the sun are, every one,
   My chargers for the field.

The morning gives me golden steeds,
   The moon gives silver-white ;
The stars drop down, my helm to crown,
   When I go forth to fight.

Against me ride in iron mail
   The squadrons of the foe :
The bucklers flash, the maces crash,
   The haughty trumpets blow.

One touch, and all, with armor cleft,
   Before me turn and yield.
Straight on I ride : the world is wide ;
   A rose-leaf is my shield !

Then dances o'er the water-fall
   The rainbow, in its glee ;

The daisy sings, the lily rings
  Her bells of victory.

So am I armed where'er I go,
  And mounted, night or day:
Who shall oppose the conquering rose,
  And who the sunbeam slay?

VII.

The star o' the morn is whitest,
The bosom of dawn is brightest;
  The dew is sown,
  And the blossom blown
Wherein thou, my Dear, delightest!

Hark, I have risen before thee,
That the spell of the day be o'er thee;
  That the flush of my love
  May fall from above,
And, mixed with the morn, adore thee!

Dark dreams must now forsake thee,
And the bliss of thy being take thee!

Let the beauty of morn
In thine eyes be born,
And the thought of me awake thee !

Come forth to hear thy praises,
Which the wakening world upraises;
Let thy hair be spun
With the gold o' the sun,
And thy feet be kissed by the daisies !

VIII.

Near in the forest
I know a glade ;
Under the tree-tops
A secret shade !

Vines are the curtains,
Blossoms the floor ;
Voices of waters
Sing evermore.

There, when the sunset's
Lances of gold

Pierce, or the moonlight
 Is silvery cold,

Would that an angel
 Led thee to me —
So, out of loneliness
 Love should be !

Never the breezes
 Should lisp what we say,
Never the waters
 Our secret betray !

Silence and shadow,
 After, might reign ;
But the old life be ours
 Never again !

CANOPUS.

A LEAF FROM THE PAST.

ABOVE the palms, the peaks of pearly gray
    That hang, like dreams, along the slumbering skies,
An urn of fire that never burns away,
        I see Canopus rise.

An urn of light, a golden-hearted torch,
    Voluptuous, drowsy-throbbing mid the stars,
As, incense-fed, from Aphrodite's porch
        Lifted, to beacon Mars.

Is it from songs and stories of the Past,
    With names and scenes that make our planet fair, —
From Babylonian splendors, vague and vast,
        And flushed Arabian air : —

Or sprung from richer longings of the brain
    And spices of the blood, this hot desire
To lie beneath that mellow lamp again
    And breathe its languid fire?

From tales of nights when watching David saw
    Its amorous ray on bright Bathsheba's head;
Or Charmian stole, the golden gauze to draw
    Round Cleopatra's bed?

Or when white-breasted Paris touched the lone
    Laconian isle, where stayed his flying oars,
And Helen breathed the scent of violets, blown
    Along the bosky shores?

Or Kalidasa's maiden, wandering through
    The moonlit jungles of the Indian lands,
While shamed mimosas from her form withdrew
    Their thin and trembling hands?

For Fancy takes from Passion power to build
    A brighter fane than bloodless Thought decrees,
And loves to see its spacious chambers filled
    With tropic tapestries.

And, past those halls which for itself the mind
    Builds, permanent as marble, and as cold,
In warm surprises of the blood we find
      The sumptuous dream unfold!

There shines the leaf and bursts the blossom sheath
    On hills deep-mantled in eternal June,
Or wave their whispering silver, underneath
      The rainbow-cinctured moon.

Around the pillars of the palm-tree bower
    The orchids cling, in rose and purple spheres ;
Shield-broad the lily floats ; the aloe flower
      Foredates its hundred years.

Along the lines of coral, white and warm,
    Breaks the white surf ; hushed is the glassy air,
And only mellower murmurs tell that storm
      Is raging otherwhere.

The mansion gleams with dome and arch Moresque —
    Ah, bliss to lie beside the jasper urn
Of founts, and through the open arabesque
      To watch Canopus burn !

8

To sit at feasts, and fluid odors drain
     Of daintiest nectar that from grape is caught,
While faint narcotics cheat the idle brain
          With phantom shapes of thought ;

Or, listening to the sweet, seductive voice,
     No will hath silenced, since the world began,
To weigh delight unchallenged, making choice
          Of earlier joys of man !

Permit the dream : our natures twofold are.
     Sense hath its own ideals, which prepare
A rosy background for the soul's white star,
          Whereon it shines more fair.

Not crystal runs, dissolved from mountain snow,
     The poet's blood ; but amber, musk, impart
Their scents, and gems their orbed or shivered glow,
          To feed his tropic heart.

While Form and Color undivorced remain
     In every planet gilded by the sun,
His craft shall forge the radiant marriage chain
          That makes them purely One !

1865.

CUPIDO.

THE REVIVAL OF AN ANTIQUATED FIGURE, AFTER READING THE VIEWS OF CERTAIN WOMEN ON MARRIAGE AND DIVORCE.

I.

ROSEATE darling,
Dimpled with laughter,
Nursed on the bosom
Pierced by thee after ;
Fed with the rarest
Milk of the fairest
Fond Aphrodite,
Child as thou art, as a god thou art mighty !

II.

Thou art the only
Demigod left us ;
Fate hath bereft us,
Science made lonely.

Visions and fables
Shrink from our portals ;
Long have we banished
The stately Immortals ;
Yet, when we sent them
Trooping to Hades —
Olympian gentlemen,
Paphian ladies —
Thou hadst re-risen,
Ere the dark prison
Closed for the last time,
Slipped from the gate and returned to thy pastime !

III.

Ever a mystery,
All of our history
Brightens with thee !
Systems have chained us,
Rulers restrained us,
Fortune disdained us,
Still thou wert free !
Lofty or lowly,
Brutish or holy,

Spacious or narrow,
Never a life was secure from thy arrow!

IV.

Ah, but they 've told us
Love is a system!
They would withhold us
When we have kissed him!
All that perplexes
Sweetly the sexes
They would control,
And with Affinity
Drive the Divinity
Out of the soul!
Better, they say, is
Phryne or Laïs
Than the immutable
Faith, and its suitable
Vow, he hath taught us;
Foolish the tender
Pang, the surrender,
When he has caught us;
Fancies and fetters are all he has brought us.

V.

Future parental,
Physical, mental
Laws they prescribe us ;
And with ecstatic
Strict mathematic
Blisses would bribe us.
Alkali, acid,
They with a placid
Mien would unite,
And the wild rapture
Of chasing and capture
Curb with a right ;
Measuring, dealing
Even the kiss of the twilight of feeling !

VI.

Who shall deliver
Thee from their credo ?
Rent is thy quiver,
Darling Cupido !

Naked, yet blameless,
Tricksily aimless,
Secretly sure,
Who, then, thy plighting,
Wilful uniting,
Now will endure?
Now, when expériment
Based upon Science
Sets at defiance,
Harshly, thy merriment,
Who shall caress thee
Warm in his bosom, and bliss thee and bless thee?

VII.

Ever 't is May-time!
Ever 't is play-time
Of Beauty and Youth!
Freed from confusion,
Hides in illusion
Nature her truth.
Books and discourses,
What can they tell us?
Blood with its forces

Still will compel us !

Cold ones may fly to

Systems, or try to ;

Innocent fancy

Still will enwind us,

Love's necromancy,

Snare us and bind us,

Systems and rights lie forgotten behind us.

SONNET.

WHO, harnessed in his mail of Self, demands
To be men's master and their sovran guide ? —
Proclaims his place, and by sole right of pride
A candidate for love and reverence stands,
As if the power within his empty hands
Had fallen from the sky, with all beside,
So oft to longing and to toil denied,
That makes the leaders and the lords of lands ?
He who would lead must first himself be led ;
Who would be loved be capable of love
Beyond the utmost he receives ; who claims
The rod of power must first have bowed his head,
And, being honored, honor what 's above :
This know the men who leave the world their names.

8 *   L.

FROM THE NORTH.

ONCE more without you !   Sighing, Dear, once more,
For all the sweet, accustomed ministries
Of wife and mother : not as when the seas
That parted us my tender message bore
From the gray olives of the Cretan shore
To those that hide the broken Phidian frieze
Of our Athenian home, — but far degrees,
Wide plains, great forests, part us now.   My door
Looks on the rushing Neva, cold and clear :
The swelling domes in hovering splendor lie
Like golden bubbles, eager to be gone ;
But the chill crystal of the atmosphere
Withholds them, and along the northern sky
The amber midnight smiles in dreams of dawn.

A WEDDING SONNET.

TO T. B. A. AND L. W.

SAD Autumn, drop thy weedy crown forlorn,
Put off thy cloak of cloud, thy scarf of mist,
And dress in gauzy gold and amethyst
A day benign, of sunniest influence born,
As may befit a Poet's marriage morn!
Give buds another dream, another tryst
To loving hearts, and print on lips unkissed
Betrothal-kisses, laughing Spring to scorn!
Yet, if unfriendly thou, with sullen skies,
Bleak rains, or moaning winds, dost menace wrong,
Here art thou foiled: a bridal sun shall rise
And bridal emblems unto these belong.
Round her the sunshine of her beauty lies,
And breathes round him the spring-time of his song!

CHRISTMAS SONNETS.

I.

TO G. H. B.

IF that my hand, like yours, dear George, were skilled
To win from Wordsworth's scanty plot of ground
A shining harvest, such as you have found,
Where strength and grace, fraternally fulfilled,   .
As in those sheaves whose rustling glories gild
The hills of August, folded are, and bound ;
So would I draw my loving tillage round
Its borders, bid the gentlest rains be spilled,
The goldenest suns its happy growth compel,
And bind for you the ripe, redundant grain :
But, ah ! you stand amid your songful sheaves,
So rich, this weed-born flower you might disdain,
Save that of me its growth and color tell,
And of my love some perfume haunt its leaves !

II.

TO R. H. S.

THE years go by, old Friend! Each, as it fleets,
Moves to a farther, fairer realm, the time
When first we twain the pleasant land of Rhyme
Discovered, choosing side by side our seats
Below our separate Gods: in midnight streets
And haunted attics flattered by the chime
Of silver words, and, fed by faith sublime,
I Shelley's mantle wore, you that of Keats, —
Dear dreams, that marked the Muse's childhood then,
Nor now to be disowned! The years go by;
The clear-eyed Goddess flatters us no more;
And yet, I think, in soberer aims of men,
And Song's severer service, you and I
Are nearer, dearer, faithfuller than before.

III.

WHEN days were long, and o'er that farm of mine,
Green Cedarcroft, the summer breezes blew,
And from the walnut shadows I and you,
Dear Edmund, saw the red lawn-roses shine,
Or followed our idyllic Brandywine
Through meadows flecked with many a flowery hue,
To where with wild Arcadian pomp I drew
Your Bacchic march among the startled kine,
You gave me, linked with old Mæonides,
Your loving sonnet, — record dear and true
Of days as dear: and now, when suns are brief,
And Christmas snows are on the naked trees,
I give you this, — a withered winter leaf,
Yet with your blossom from one root it grew.

IV.

TO J. L. G.

IF I could touch with Petrarch's pen this strain
Of graver song, and shape to liquid flow
Of soft Italian syllables the glow
That warms my heart, my tribute were not vain:
But how shall I such measured sweetness gain
As may your golden nature fitly show,
And with the heart-light shine, that fills you so,
It pales the graces of the cultured brain?
Long have I known, Love better is than Fame,
And Love hath crowned you: yet if any bay
Cling to my chaplet when the years have fled,
And I am dust, may this which bears your name
Cling latest, that my love's result shall stay
When that which mine ambition wrought is dead!

A STATESMAN.

HE knew the mask of principle to wear,
And power accept while seeming to decline:
So cunningly he wrought, with tools so fine,
Setting his courses with so frank an air,
(Yet most secure when seeming most to dare,)
He did deceive us all: with mien benign
His malice smiled, his cowardice the sign
Of courage took, his selfishness grew fair,
So deftly could his foiled ambition show
As modest acquiescence.   Now, 't is clear
What man he is, — how false his high report ;
Mean to the friend, caressing to the foe ;
Plotting the mischief which he feigns to fear :
Chief Eunuch, were but ours the Sultan's court !

ODES.

ODES.

GETTYSBURG ODE.

DEDICATION OF THE NATIONAL MONUMENT, JULY 1, 1869.

I.

AFTER the eyes that looked, the lips that spake
Here, from the shadows of impending death,
    Those words of solemn breath,
    What voice may fitly break
The silence, doubly hallowed, left by him?
We can but bow the head, with eyes grown dim,
    And, as a Nation's litany, repeat
The phrase his martyrdom hath made complete,
Noble as then, but now more sadly-sweet :
" Let us, the Living, rather dedicate
Ourselves to the unfinished work, which they
Thus far advanced so nobly on its way,
    And save the perilled State!

Let us, upon this field where they, the brave,

Their last full measure of devotion gave,

Highly resolve they have not died in vain ! —

That, under God, the Nation's later birth

　　Of Freedom, and the people's gain

Of their own Sovereignty, shall never wane

And perish from the circle of the earth ! "

From such a perfect text, shall Song aspire

　　To light her faded fire,

　　And into wandering music turn

Its virtue, simple, sorrowful and stern ?

His voice all elegies anticipated ;

　　For, whatsoe'er the strain,

　　We hear that one refrain :

" We consecrate ourselves to them, the Consecrated ! "

II.

After the thunder-storm our heaven is blue :

　Far-off, along the borders of the sky,

　In silver folds the clouds of battle lie,

With soft, consoling sunlight shining through ;

And round the sweeping circle of your hills

　　The crashing cannon-thrills

Have faded from the memory of the air ;
And Summer pours from unexhausted fountains
    Her bliss on yonder mountains :
The camps are tenantless, the breastworks bare :
Earth keeps no stain where hero-blood was poured :
  The hornets, humming on their wings of lead,
  Have ceased to sting, their angry swarms are dead,
And, harmless in its scabbard, rusts the sword !

III.

O, not till now, — O, now we dare, at last,
  To give our heroes fitting consecration !
Not till the soreness of the strife is past,
  And Peace hath comforted the weary Nation !
So long her sad, indignant spirit held
One keen regret, one throb of pain, unquelled ;
So long the land about her feet was waste,
  The ashes of the burning lay upon her,
We stood beside their graves with brows abased,
  Waiting the purer mood to do them honor !
They, through the flames of this dread holocaust,
The patriot's wrath, the soldier's ardor, lost :

They sit above us and above our passion,

    Disparaged even by our human tears, —-

Beholding truth our race, perchance, may fashion

    In the slow process of the creeping years.

We saw the still reproof upon their faces ;

We heard them whisper from the shining spaces :

" To-day ye grieve : come not to us with sorrow !

Wait for the glad, the reconciled To-morrow !

Your grief but clouds the ether where we dwell ;

    Your anger keeps your souls and ours apart :

But come with peace and pardon, all is well !

    And come with love, we touch you, heart to heart ! "

IV.

    Immortal Brothers, we have heard !

Our lips declare the reconciling word :

For Battle taught, that set us face to face,

    The stubborn temper of the race,

And both, from fields no longer alien, come,

    To grander action equally invited, —

Marshalled by Learning's trump, by Labor's drum,

    In strife that purifies and makes united !

We force to build, the powers that would destroy ;

The muscles, hardened by the sabre's grasp,
  Now give our hands a firmer clasp:
We bring not grief to you, but solemn joy!
    And, feeling you so near,
Look forward with your eyes, divinely clear,
To some sublimely-perfect, sacred year,
When sons of fathers whom ye overcame
Forget in mutual pride the partial blame,
And join with us, to set the final crown
    Upon your dear renown, —
The People's Union in heart and name!

V.

    And yet, ye Dead! — and yet
Our clouded natures cling to one regret:
    We are not all resigned
    To yield, with even mind,
Our scarcely-risen stars, that here untimely set.
We needs must think of History that waits
  For lines that live but in their proud beginning, —
Arrested promises and cheated fates, —
  Youth's boundless venture and its single winning!

We see the ghosts of deeds they might have done,

 The phantom homes that beaconed their endeavor;

The seeds of countless lives, in them begun,

 That might have multiplied for us forever!

  We grudge the better strain of men

That proved itself, and was extinguished then —

The field, with strength and hope so thickly sown,

Wherefrom no other harvest shall be mown :

For all the land, within its clasping seas,

 Is poorer now in bravery and beauty,

Such wealth of manly loves and energies

Was given to teach us all the free man's sacred duty!

VI.

  Again 't is they, the Dead,

  By whom our hearts are comforted.

Deep as the land-blown murmurs of the waves

The answer cometh from a thousand graves :

 " Not so! we are not orphaned of our fate !

Though life were warmest and though love were sweetest,

We still have portion in their best estate :

 Our fortune is the fairest and completest !

Our homes are everywhere: our loves are set

   In hearts of man and woman, sweet and vernal:

Courage and Truth, the children we beget,

   Unmixed of baser earth, shall be eternal.

A finer spirit in the blood shall give

The token of the lines wherein we live, —

Unselfish force, unconscious nobleness

   That in the shocks of fortune stands unshaken, —

The hopes that in their very being bless,

   The aspirations that to deeds awaken!

If aught of finer virtue ye allow

   To us, that faith alone its like shall win you;

So, trust like ours shall ever lift the brow;

   And strength like ours shall ever steel the sinew!

We are the blossoms which the storm has cast

   From the Spring promise of our Freedom's tree,

Pruning its overgrowths, that so, at last,

   Its later fruit more bountiful shall be! —

Content, if, when the balm of Time assuages

The branch's hurt, some fragrance of our lives

     In all the land survives,

And makes their memory sweet through still expanding

    ages!"

9   M

VII.

Thus grandly, they we mourn, themselves console us ;

And, as their spirits conquer and control us,

We hear, from some high realm that lies beyond,

The hero-voices of the Past respond.

From every State that reached a broader right

Through fiery gates of battle ; from the shock

Of old invasions on the People's rock ;

From tribes that stood, in Kings' and Priests' despite ;

From graves, forgotten in the Syrian sand,

Or nameless barrows of the Northern strand,

Or gorges of the Alps and Pyrenees,

Or the dark bowels of devouring seas, —

Wherever Man for Man's sake died, — wherever

Death stayed the march of upward-climbing feet,

    Leaving their Present incomplete,

But through far Futures crowning their endeavor, —

Their ghostly voices to our ears are sent,

As when the high note of a trumpet wrings

    Æolian answers from the strings

Of many a mute, unfingered instrument !

Platæan cymbals thrill for us to-day ;

The horns of Sempach in our echoes play,

And nearer yet, and sharper, and more stern,
The slogan rings that startled Bannockburn ;
Till from the field, made green with kindred deed,
   The shields are clashed in exultation
      Above the dauntless Nation,
That for a Continent has fought its Runnymede !

VIII.

Ay, for a Continent !   The heart that beats
   With such rich blood of sacrifice
Shall, from the Tropics, drowsed with languid heats,
   To the blue ramparts of the Northern ice,
Make felt its pulses, all this young world over ! —
      Shall thrill, and shake, and sway
Each land that bourgeons in the Western day,
Whatever flag may float, whatever shield may cover !
   With fuller manhood every wind is rife,
      In every soil are sown the seeds of valor,
Since out of death came forth such boundless life,
      Such ruddy beauty out of anguished pallor !
   And that first deed, along the southern wave,
      Spoiled not the sister-land, but lent an arm to save !

IX.

Now, in her seat secure,
Where distant menaces no more can reach her,
　　Our land, in undivided freedom pure,
Becomes the unwilling world's unconscious teacher ;
And, day by day, beneath serener skies,
The unshaken pillars of her palace rise, —
The Doric shafts, that lightly upward press,
And hide in grace their giant massiveness.
What though the sword has hewn each corner-stone,
　　And precious blood cements the deep foundation !
Never by other force have empires grown ;
　　From other basis never rose a nation !
For strength is born of struggle, faith of doubt,
　　Of discord law, and freedom of oppression :
We hail from Pisgah, with exulting shout,
The Promised Land below us, bright with sun,
　　　　And deem its pastures won,
Ere toil and blood have earned us their possession !
Each aspiration of our human earth
Becomes an act through keenest pangs of birth ;
Each force, to bless, must cease to be a dream,
And conquer life through agony supreme ;

Each inborn right must outwardly be tested
   By stern material weapons, ere it stand
   In the enduring fabric of the land,
Secured for those who yielded it, and those who wrested !

X.

'This they have done for us who slumber here, —
   Awake, alive, though now so dumbly sleeping ;
Spreading the board, but tasting not its cheer,
     Sowing, but never reaping ; —
Building, but never sitting in the shade
Of the strong mansion they have made ; —
Speaking their word of life with mighty tongue,
But hearing not the echo, million-voiced,
     Of brothers who rejoiced,
From all our river vales and mountains flung !
So take them, Heroes of the songful Past !
Open your ranks, let every shining troop
     Its phantom banners droop,
To hail Earth's noblest martyrs, and her last !
     Take them, O Fatherland !
   Who, dying, conquered in thy name ;
     And, with a grateful hand,

Inscribe their deed who took away thy blame, —
Give, for their grandest all, thine insufficient fame !
    Take them, O God ! our Brave,
  The glad fulfillers of Thy dread decree ;
  Who grasped the sword for Peace, and smote to save,
And, dying here for Freedom, also died for Thee !

SHAKESPEARE'S STATUE.

CENTRAL PARK, NEW YORK, MAY 23, 1872.

I.

IN this free Pantheon of the air and sun,
Where stubborn granite grudgingly gives place
To petted turf, the garden's daintier race
　　Of flowers, and Art hath slowly won
A smile from grim, primeval barrenness,
　　　　What alien Form doth stand?
Where scarcely yet the heroes of the land,
As in their future's haven, from the stress
Of all conflicting tides, find quiet deep
　　　　Of bronze or marble sleep,
What stranger comes, to join the scanty band?
　　Who pauses here, as one that muses
　　While centuries of men go by,
　　And unto all our questioning refuses
　　His clear, infallible reply?
Who hath his will of us, beneath our new-world sky?

II.

Here, in his right, he stands !
No breadth of earth-dividing seas can bar
The breeze of morning, or the morning star,
From visiting our lands :
His wit, the breeze, his wisdom, as the star,
Shone where our earliest life was set, and blew
To freshen hope and plan
In brains American, —
To urge, resist, encourage, and subdue !
He came, a household ghost we could not ban :
He sat, on winter nights, by cabin-fires ;
His summer fairies linked their hands
Along our yellow sands ;
He preached within the shadow of our spires ;
And when the certain Fate drew nigh, to cleave
The birth-cord, and a separate being leave,
He, in our ranks of patient-hearted men,
Wrought with the boundless forces of his fame,
Victorious, and became
The Master of our thought, the land's first Citizen !

III.

If, here, his image seem
Of softer scenes and grayer skies to dream,
Thatched cot and rustic tavern, ivied hall,
 The cuckoo's April call
And cowslip-meads beside the Avon stream,
He shall not fail that other home to find
 We could not leave behind!
The forms of Passion, which his fancy drew,
 In us their ancient likenesses beget;
So, from our lives forever born anew,
 He stands amid his own creations yet!
Here comes lean Cassius, of conventions tired;
 Here, in his coach, luxurious Antony
Beside his Egypt, still of men admired;
 And Brutus plans some purer liberty!
A thousand Shylocks, Jew and Christian, pass;
 A hundred Hamlets, by their times betrayed;
And sweet Anne Page comes tripping o'er the grass,
 And antlered Falstaff pants beneath the shade.
Here toss upon the wanton summer wind
 The locks of Rosalind;

9*

Here some gay glove the damnéd spot conceals
    Which Lady Macbeth feels:
His ease here smiling smooth Iago takes,
  And outcast Lear gives passage to his woe,
And here some foiled Reformer sadly breaks
      His wand of Prospero!
    In liveried splendor, side by side,
    Nick Bottom and Titania ride;
    And Portia, flushed with cheers of men,
    Disdains dear, faithful Imogen;
    And Puck, beside the form of Morse,
    Stops on his forty-minute course;
    And Ariel from his swinging bough
    A blossom casts on Bryant's brow,
Until, as summoned from his brooding brain,
    He sees his children all again,
In us, as on our lips, each fresh, immortal strain!

        IV.

Be welcome, Master! In our active air
Keep the calm strength we need to learn of thee!
    A steadfast anchor be
Mid passions that exhaust, and times that wear!

Thy kindred race, that scarcely knows
What power is in Repose,
What permanence in Patience, what renown
In silent faith and plodding toil of Art
That shyly works apart,
All these in thee unconsciously doth crown!

V.

The Many grow, through honor to the One;
And what of loftier life we do not live,
This Form shall help to give,
In our free Pantheon of the air and sun!
Here, where the noise of Trade is loudest,
It builds a shrine august,
To show, while pomp of wealth is proudest,
How brief is gilded dust:
How Art succeeds, though long,
And o'er the tumult of the generations,
The strong, enduring spirit of the nations,
How speaks the voice of Song!
Our City, at her gateways of the sea,
Twines bay around the mural crown upon her,
And wins new grace and dearer dignity,

Giving our race's Poet honor!

If such as he

Again may ever be,

And our humanity another crown

Find in some equal, late renown,

The reverence of what he was shall call it down!

GOETHE.

I.

WHOSE voice shall so invade the spheres
That, ere it die, the Master hears?
    Whose arm is now so strong
To fling the votive garland of a song,
That some fresh odor of a world he knew
    With large enjoyment, and may yet
        Not utterly forget,
Shall reach his place, and whisper whence it grew?
    Dare we invoke him, that he pause
On trails divine of unimagined laws,
    And bend the luminous eyes
Experience could not dim, nor Fate surprise,
On these late honors, where we fondly seem,
Him thus exalting, like him to aspire,
    And reach, in our desire,
The triumph of his toil, the beauty of his dream!

II.

God moulds no second poet from the clay
Time once hath cut in marble : when, at last,
    The veil is plucked away,
We see no face familiar to the Past.
   New mixtures of the elements,
And fresh espousals of the soul and sense,
    At first disguise
The unconjectured Genius to our eyes,
Till self-nursed faith and self encouraged power
    Win the despotic hour
That bids our doubting race accept and recognize !

III.

Ah, who shall say what cloud of disregard,
  Cast by the savage ancient fame
    Of some forgotten name,
    Mantled the Chian bard?
He walked beside the strong, prophetic sea,
Indifferent as itself, and nobly free ;
While roll of waves and rhythmic sound of oars
    Along Ionian shores,

To Troy's high story chimed in undertone,

And gave his song the accent of their own!

What classic ghost severe was summoned up

To threaten Dante, when the bitter bread

    Of exile on his board was spread,

The bitter wine of bounty filled his cup?

We need not ask : the unpropitious years,

    The hate of Guelf, the lordly sneers

Of Della Scala's court, the Roman ban,

      Were but as eddying dust

      To his firm-centred trust ;

    For through that air without a star

Burned one unwavering beacon from afar,

That kept him his and ours, the stern, immortal man!

What courtier, stuffed with smooth, accepted lore

      Of Song's patrician line,

But shrugged his velvet shoulders all the more,

    And heard, with bland indulgent face,

    As who bestows a grace,

The homely phrase that Shakespeare made divine?

    So, now, the dainty souls that crave

Light stepping-stones across a shallow wave,

Shrink from the deeps of Goethe's soundless song !

    So, now, the weak, imperfect fire

That knows but half of passion and desire
Betrays itself, to do the Master wrong ; —
Turns, dazzled by his white, uncolored glow,
And deems his sevenfold heat the wintry flash of snow !

IV.

Fate, like a grudging child,
Herself once reconciled
To power by loss, by suffering to fame ;
Weighing the Poet's name
With blindness, exile, want, and aims denied ;
Or let faint spirits perish in their pride ;
Or gave her justice when its need had died ;
But as if weary she
Of struggle crowned by victory,
Him with the largesse of her gifts she tried !
Proud beauty to the boy she gave :
A lip that bubbled song, yet lured the bee ;
An eye of light, a forehead pure and free ;
Strength as of streams, and grace as of the wave !
Round him the morning air
Of life she charmed, and made his pathway fair ;
Lent Love her lightest chain,

That laid no bondage on the haughty brain,
And cheapened honors with a new disdain :
 Kept, through the shocks of Time,
For him the haven of a peace sublime,
 And let his sight forerun
The sown achievement, to the harvest won !

V.

 But Fortune's darling stood unspoiled :
  Caressing Love and Pleasure,
He let not go the imperishable treasure :
He thought, and sported ; carolled free, and toiled :
He stretched wide arms to clasp the joy of Earth,
  But delved in every field
 Of knowledge, conquering all clear worth
Of action, that ennobles through the sense
  Of wholly used intelligence :
From loftiest pinnacles, that shone revealed
In pure poetic ether, he could bend
  To win the little store
  Of humblest Labor's lore,
And give each face of Life the greeting of a friend !
 He taught, and governed, — knew the thankless days

Of service and dispraise ;
He followed Science on her stony ways ;
    He turned from princely state, to heed
        The single nature's need,
    And, through the chill of hostile years,
Never unlearned the noble shame of tears!
Faced by fulfilled Ideals, he aspired
To win the perished secret of their grace, —
To dower the earnest children of a race
Toil never tamed, nor acquisition tired,
With Freedom born of Beauty ! — and for them
        His Titan soul combined
        The passions of the mind,
Which blood and time so long had held apart,
Till the white blossom of the Grecian Art
The world saw shine once more, upon a Gothic stem !

VI.

    His measure would we mete ?
It is a sea that murmurs at our feet.
    Wait, first, upon the strand :
A far shore glimmers — " knowest thou the land?"
Whence these gay flowers that breathe beside the water ?

Ask thou the Erl-King's daughter!
It is no cloud that darkens thus the shore :
   Faust on his mantle passes o'er.
   The water roars, the water heaves,
     The trembling waves divide :
   A shape of beauty, rising, cleaves
     The green translucent tide.
The shape is a charm, the voice is a spell ;
We yield, and dip in the gentle swell.
Then billowy arms our limbs entwine,
And, chill as the hidden heat of wine,
We meet the shock of the sturdy brine ;
And we feel, beneath the surface-flow,
The tug of the powerful undertow,
     That ceaselessly gathers and sweeps
To broader surges and darker deeps ;
Till, faint and breathless, we can but float
Idly, and listen to many a note
From horns of the Tritons flung afar ;
     And see, on the watery rim,
     The circling Dorides swim,
And Cypris, poised on her dove-drawn car !
     Torn from the deepest caves,
     Sea-blooms brighten the waves :

The breaker throws pearls on the sand,
And inlets pierce to the heart of the land,
        Winding by dorf and mill,
    Where the shores are green and the waters still,
        And the force, but now so wild,
Mirrors the maiden and sports with the child!
    Spent from the sea, we gain its brink,
        With soul aroused and limbs aflame:
Half are we drawn, and half we sink,
        But rise no more the same.

VII.

O meadows threaded by the silver Main!
        O Saxon hills of pine,
Witch-haunted Hartz, and thou,
        Deep vale of Ilmenau!
Ye knew your poet; and not only ye:
        The purple Tyrrhene Sea
Not murmurs Virgil less, but him the more;
        The Lar of haughty Rome
        Gave the high guest a home:
He dwells with Tasso on Sorrento's shore!
The dewy wild-rose of his German lays,

Beside the classic cyclamen,
   In many a Sabine glen,
  Sweetens the calm Italian days.
But pass the hoary ridge of Lebanon,
   To where the sacred sun
Beams on Schiráz ; and lo ! before the gates,
  Goethe, the heir of Hafiz, waits.
Know ye the turbaned brow, the Persian guise,
The bearded lips, the deep yet laughing eyes ?
    A cadence strange and strong
    Fills each voluptuous song,
And kindles energy from old repose ;
    Even as first, amid the throes
     Of the unquiet West,
He breathed repose to heal the old unrest !

VIII.

Dear is the Minstrel, yet the Man is more ;
But should I turn the pages of his brain,
The lighter muscle of my verse would strain
    And break beneath his lore.
How charge with music powers so vast and free,
   Save one be great as he ?

Behold him, as ye jostle with the throng

Through narrow ways, that do your beings wrong, —

    Self chosen lanes, wherein ye press

       In louder Storm and Stress,

    Passing the lesser bounty by

    Because the greater seems too high,

    And that sublimest joy forego,

       To seek, aspire, and know!

Behold in him, since our strong line began,

       The first full-statured man !

Dear is the Minstrel, even to hearts of prose ;

But he who sets all aspiration free

       Is dearer to humanity.

Still through our age the shadowy Leader goes ;

Still whispers cheer, or waves his warning sign ;

       The man who, most of men,

Heeded the parable from lips divine,

       And made one talent ten !

THE END.

Cambridge : Electrotyped and Printed by **Welch,** Bigelow, & Co.